S&B RANCH PUBLISHING

PRESENTS

A SAINT RENEE PRODUCTION

CAPTAIN

COWBOY

FIRST EDITION

BY WILLIAM J. CHAMBERS MSed.

AND SUSAN R. HAIRRELL

EDITED BY GLORY ANN KURTZ

S&S RANCH PUBLISHING
BOYD, TEXAS

P.O. BOX 1338
76023

COPYRIGHT @ WILLIAM J. CHAMBERS 2011

ALL RIGHTS RESERVED

2

DEDICATION

Jerald Steven Rogers was many things to many people.
He was a son, a dad, a brother, and a husband.
Many of us saw different things in him. I saw a sea-man.
I saw my Captain. I wrote this book in his memory
knowing full well I could not do justice to the man.

Calm winds and fair seas, Captain Rogers
Just roll with the waves.
If I ain't sinking, I must be swimming
If I ain't dead, I must be living.
And it's living that scares me the most.
If I ain't sleeping, hell let's go fishing.
If I ain't anchored, I will be drifting.
LJT

FORWARD

William Chambers has written a colorful, witty story about Bubba Lee McBride, who was born a five-generation rancher running cattle on a piece of Texas earth. However, with the loss of his parents and the ranch, he spent the first part of his life trying to figure out how to get the ranch back.

But that all changed when he and his sister, Sherry, decided to fulfill their new dreams by moving to a Caribbean island. Hers was to own a restaurant; his was to become a sea captain and he soon affectionately became known as Captain Cowboy by those in the small island town.

As fate would have it, he and his faithful dog, Jester, got lost in a wild hurricane and shipwrecked on a remote Caribbean island. It seemed like he was destined to spend the rest of his life there alone, but as luck would have it, it was there that he found the love of his life.

Chambers has woven situations into this book that can make you laugh, make you cry and surprise you in pages filled with twists and turns. Chambers has the unique ability to transform a cowboy into a sea captain, giving you a story that won't let you put this book down until you've read each and every page.

Glory Ann Kurtz

TABLE OF CONTENTS

CARIBBEAN DREAMING

Chapter 1

Bubba Lee McBride and his faithful dog, Jester, stood on the docks of a small island awaiting a sea plane he had chartered two days earlier. The man with a one-hundred-twenty-pound dog on one side of him and a duffle bag on the other, could not believe how far he had come in such a short time. "Life was truly a carnival," as the Caribbean people proved almost daily.

A few months earlier he had been the foreman on the ranch he had grown up on. A life he was made for, yet somehow his heart had always longed for the sea. A few situations and circumstances conspired to form his present and future. The next thing Bubba knew, he was bound for the adventure of a lifetime. In a very short time, he had gone from a West Texas ranch hand to an expatriate American.

Looking back on it, the origin of the man's mid-life's crisis was a story penned by Jimmy Buffett. Buffett's tale was about a Wyoming cowboy named Tully Mars and his horse Mr. Twain. Tully had become somewhat of an outlaw after offending the new owners of the ranch he worked on. Something about throwing a message table through a ten-thousand-dollar, plate-glass window would do the trick every time.

Tully headed south toward the Gulf of Mexico with the fuzz and a bounty hunter or two in hot pursuit. All that the Wyoming cowboy had to his name was his truck and horse trailer, Mr. Twain and a comp shell given to him by an old Indian. The adventures that followed Tully and Mr. Twain got Bubba Lee to thinking, and then real life began to imitate art.

The thirty-seven-year old Bubba Lee knew life wasn't as simple as a story in a book, but in his way of thinking, it should be. He and the character Tully Mars had a lot in common: all but a horse named Mr. Twain. Bubba had Jester and he was damn near as big as a horse. The ledger seemed to even out on that measure alone.

Shortly after Bubba read the short story about the wanted Wyoming cowboy, a blizzard hit the West Texas Plains. The mercury fell about as fast as the price of Texas sweet crude on the recent market. Texas was in a deep freeze, both figuratively and financially. The prospects for the Lone Star State weren't looking all that shiny. Boom or bust - that was the true nature of the state, and Bubba was looking for the off ramp.

It happened at the end of a long, hard, freezing day. Anything that could go wrong did. Jester came up missing just about the time Bubba was fixing to call it a day. Some of the boys on the ranch thought it would be funny to highjack the foreman's dog and go bar hopping. Jester always had a taste for whiskey; that was a well-known fact.

Bubba was not a happy camper when he found his dog that night. Jester on the other hand, well he was quite happy. The dog's owner was tired, mad, and half frozen by the time he made it back to the ranch. He built a fire, made a pot of coffee and grabbed Buffett's book of short stories off the shelf.

Bubbe Lee kicked back in his old easy chair with a blanket and began to read. It wasn't long before the day's hard work finally caught up with the cowboy and he was fast asleep.

Bubba dreamed the dream of a lifetime that night. He and his old mutt had been awakened in the middle of the storm by one of the hands. It was the boss's prize winning bull; he had escaped in the storm.

In Bubba's dream, he and Jester chased the owner's high-dollar hamburger stand all the way to the Florida Keys. Bubba sold the bull and bought a charter boat as soon as he corralled the damn thing. The dream was a little farfetched but, what the hell, it was a dream after all. The dream did more than bring a smile to the man's face; it planted a seed.

A year had passed like the proverbial sands through an hourglass. Only two things were certain in the cowboy's sphere: the recession in Texas had not found its bottom and Bubba's thoughts of the sea were alive and well.

Up until the real crash, Bubba's thoughts of the islands were just that: thoughts. A toy to be taken out and played with when the night became too lonely and the days seemed too long. They were fantasies of a man nearing middle age, if you will. The regimental and rigid life of a cowboy always seemed more like a prison to him. It was up before dawn, and early to his bunk at the end of the day. The rules he had grown up with seemed to be slowly killing the man inside.

He could have thrown caution to the wind but the life of a simple cowboy seemed to be ingrained in his very nature: five generations of McBrides had run cattle on that piece of Texas earth. It would be him running his cattle on his land if not for the loss of his parents, as well as the loss of the ranch when another boom long ago went bust.

It seemed like three-fourths of his life had been spent trying to figure out how to get the family ranch back. Finally the realization set in that the best he could ever hope for was to be the foreman on a ranch that once bore his family's name. He might have left after the realization set in if not for another factor.

Sherry Riddle was more or less Bubba's adopted sister. Her family had looked after the small boy after his father had, in a fit of depression, taken his own life. They would have adopted the six-year-old boy but they couldn't keep him away from the ranch. Mr. Riddle, Sherry's father, would put the boy down for the night only to wake up and find him gone the next morning.

It was understood when the ranch sold that Bubba Lee and the old Mexican cook, Peto, came with the deal. The very best the Riddles could hope for was to help look out after the child. Bubba wasn't much of a child by then; too many heartaches in a life barely lived had robbed him of the innocence of childhood.

Sherry had a calming effect over the older Bubba from the start. The day John Riddle told the six-year-old boy that his father had gone to be with his mother was the first example of that. Bubba did not cry a single tear after hearing the news; he sat in the floor with a two-year-old Sherry and played with her the rest of the afternoon. The young boy did not play out of disrespect for his dead father; rather he

10

clung to Sherry as though she was the only one who understood his pain.

The bond between the two grew stronger as the years drifted by. It was Sherry, not the girl he would someday marry, who wrote him every day he was in Vietnam. Bubba knew if not for her letters, he would have never made it through two tours of Nam. Too many young men broke because they had nothing to cling to. Sergeant Bubba McBride saw it every day he was in country.

However, Bubba's real nightmare did not begin until after he rotated back to the world. He married his high school sweetheart and things went downhill after that. The two had grown apart the two years Bubba had been gone. The only time they saw each other during that time was on Bubba's first leave from boot camp. The rare times he would get leave after that, she would always find an excuse not to show up. Sherry, on the other hand, was as trustworthy and dependable as a Swiss clock. Rain or shine, if Bubba called, she was there.

It only took a little more than a year for the wheels to fall off of Bubba's marriage. The simple fact was that Bubba loved her, and she loved every other man but him. Sherry saw the train wreck coming from a mile up the track, but not poor, old Bubba. He had stumbled very few times in his life; that was just the over achiever he was. But when Bubba did fall, it was one hell of a crash.

The young man, who was hard pressed to find a bronc he couldn't ride, and a man who had walked through the fires of hell in Southeast Asia was reduced to absolutely nothing by five words, "I don't love you anymore."

Bubba Lee climbed into a bottle and stayed there for the next year of his life. He might have still been there if not for the love of Sherry. Like all pure-bred drunks, the hard-nosed cowboy finally hit bottom. Sherry was the one he reached out for when that time came.

She sobered and cleaned him up; that is after she had given him a loud and direct piece of her mind. She stayed with him until he had shaken all the poison out of his body and could function as a person again. She did something next that he could never repay her for; she gave him a puppy - a puppy that had grown into the big-ass mutt that stood beside him on the dock. Sherry was sure enough family but Jester was the best friend he ever had.

It was Sherry and with all that she meant to him, that kept him from running off and chasing a foolish dream that had came to him through the words of a fifty-year-old pirate novelist and a crazy-ass dream he had one night.

Early one spring morning, all that changed for Bubba. He was out in the barn getting his top horse ready for the day's work, which was the same thing he had done the day before and the day before that. Even though he couldn't feel it at the moment, that day would change his life forever.

The cowboy was just about to saddle the horse up when one of the hands came running into the barn.

"Bubba you got a phone call up at headquarters. I think it's Sherry," the man reported to his foreman.

"Tell her I'll call her back when I get done in here," Bubba said, directing the man to convey his message.

"You don't understand Bubba, she's crying," said the cowhand, filling in the picture a little clearer for Bubba.

"Damn it, why didn't you say so? Here, you come finish Goose," Bubba ordered.

Bubba Lee knew something had to be desperately wrong. In all the years he had known her, he could count on one hand the number of times she had called him crying. Sherry was not a cry-at-the-drop-of-a-hat type woman; it just wasn't her. So Bubba paid good mind to her on those rarest of times.

"You hang this up when I get the one in my office," Bubba told a cowboy in the main room.

The ranch foreman's office was a cluttered-up mess. Years of *Horse Reports*, *Western Horsemen* and like-minded publications were stacked haphazardly everywhere. He doubted if he had read half of them but they kept coming and he kept piling them up. He'd be damn lucky to find the phone but if Sherry was crying, it was not a conversation he wanted to have in front the rest of the hands.

"Alright, I got it now," Bubba yelled. Shortly thereafter he heard a click, letting him know the receiver in the main room had been hung up.

"What's up, little sister?" he asked as though nothing was wrong.

"They fired him, the son-of-a-bitches fired him," She cried.

"Who got fired, Sherry," a confused Bubba wanted to know.

"Daddy, down at the bank," she answered through her tears.

"Who the hell fired him? Ain't he the bank's president? How the hell does that happen?" an even more confused Bubba asked.

"The board of directors; they had meeting last night and called him this morning. They didn't even have the balls to tell him in person," She reported, her temper coming out more than her tears.

"Did they give him a reason," was the only question he could come up with.

"They said he was dragging his feet calling in people's notes," she answered.

It all started making sense to Bubba. The state of affairs in Texas wasn't all that great, and their small town wasn't the exception. Like always, people had over extended themselves when times were good. Now that times were hard, the chickens were coming home to roost.

Most people see an asshole behind a desk when they look at the president of a bank. The never realize that a man in that position feels everyone's pain. The long and short of it was, John Riddle had become a scapegoat for everyone: the people who were his best friends when they needed a loan and those on the board of directors. Bubba felt bad for Sherry's father and a little responsible.

Perhaps Mr. Riddle was slow in calling in the notes because of what happened to Bubba's own father. John Riddle and the elder McBride had been best friends since high school. Bubba's real name was John Lee, a tribute to his father's friend.

Years earlier cow prices hit an all-time low and stayed there for what seemed to be forever. The blizzard of the century then hit the ranching community, killing every cow the McBride family owned. Bubba's father lost both his legs in the storm as well. Two days before the bank called in the note on the McBride place, Bubba's father shot himself in the head. Bubba had always had the feeling that somehow John Riddle blamed himself for his best friend's actions

Another thought hit Bubba as he was mulling the situation over. Sherry also worked at the bank and had since graduated from college. He was almost afraid to ask what her reaction had been after hearing the news. Sherry was anything but a shrinking violet; she could chunk cuss words with the best of them.

"Sherry I hate to ask, but where are you calling me from?" Bubba said, interrupting her in the middle of her story.

"From home! I put in a call of my own. I told those silly bastards what they could do with their damn job." Her answer made Bubba's fears came true.

"Sherry, let me get the boys out here lined out and then I'll come over and we'll figure it out together. And please don't put in anymore phone calls. Remember we can only put out one fire at a time," Bubba joked about it, knowing it might not have been the best time for a wise-ass remark but felt a little humor couldn't hurt.

On the way over to Sherry's house, Bubba started talking out loud, as though he was talking to Jester. Some folks might have thought, "That McBride boy finally went around the bend," if they actually saw what was going on. Bubba Lee had long since given up caring what the hell people thought. Life was just too short for all that bullshit.

"I wonder what Mr, Riddle will do now?" was one of the questions he asked himself. Bubba couldn't bring himself to call the man by his first name, not even when he was by himself, even though he had known the man all his life. It wasn't that Riddle was distant or cold towards him; it was purely out of respect. He could not love or respect a man anymore. Since he couldn't call him dad, Mr. Riddle worked well.

"He'll be fine; he was going to retire next year anyway. He can get an early jump on it now," Bubba told himself, remembering a conversation he and Riddle had the previous year. Sherry's father

17

shared with Bubba that he wanted to buy an RV and travel. The job of bank president kept him tied down for the last thirty years. The only time he did get away was on bank business. Because of the events of that morning, he would have all the time in the world.

"Hell, more importantly, what's Sherry gonna do?" seemed like a more serious question. She didn't have the option of early retirement. Bubba was pretty sure there was no going back to the bank. Knowing Sherry, she had burned that bridge right down to the pylons.

He was beginning to get worried when a idea hit him. "Why not, why the hell not!" he asked himself as both a smile and a plan begin to form.

Bubba knew as he drove into her driveway that coming up with a plan would be a lot easier than getting her to go along with it. He sat in his pick-up a few minutes, trying to put together the words that would put the best face on his hair-brained scenario.

Bubba took a deep breath before ringing the doorbell. "Come on in Bubba, I'm in the kitchen, be out in a minute," he heard her voice call out from within.

Bubba walked through the door and hung his hat on a nail on the wall like he had done a million times before. He scanned the living room to see if she had made any alterations since his last visit. The momma cows back at the ranch had been calving, so he hadn't been there in awhile. Sherry was a regular homebody, always fixing up her little house. Bubba's house was a different story. As long as he had a bed, TV, his chair, and clicker, he was fine. Sherry usually was the one who did it if anything got done at his house.

Bubba didn't see any changes she might have made, but he was a man and more than likely missed it altogether. His eyes stopped when they reached the southwest corner of the room. Sherry called it Bubba's corner.

Occupying that particular space was a saddle and a few buckles he had won in his rodeo days. It was hard for Bubba Lee to believe he was ever that young. It was the thought he had every time he saw the relics of his youth. Those were some of the best days of his life, running around the country with future world champions: men like Bronc Von Kurtz and Strings Dijon. Strings had went on to meet his Creator, but every so often, he'd run into Von Kurtz.

The trophies from Bubba's short-lived rodeo career seemed to mean more to Sherry than to him. Hell, he had the stuff in storage 'til one day she found them. She asked what he was going to do with them and he up and gave the whole shooting match to her. She always figured they were sad reminders of a life that could have been.

"I'm sorry for interrupting your work, Bubba. I hope this glass of freshly brewed ice-tea will make up for a little of it," she said as she set a mason fruit jar filled with the sweet substance in front of him.

"Don't worry about that, we were just dipping cows today. You would hope they could handle that job without me," he answered in the voice she had always known.

"But still Bubba, you're the only one in the family who has a job," She said, halfway joking.

"What are you saying, everyone's going to move in with me?" he said playing along.

Bubba thought he saw a tear beginning to form in her eye as he reached for the ice-tea. He was about the only one she would let her guard down in front of; they had been through a lot together. Their bond had formed through both good and bad times. Bubba was her rock and she was his.

"Bubba, I don't know what I'm going to do. I was so mad when I made that damn phone call, I guess I just wasn't thinking," she said, beginning to sob a little.

"I thought about that too on my way over here. What would you like to do? I mean if you could do anything you wanted to do, what would it be?" Bubba asked.

She thought about his question for a moment before answering it. "I know it sounds crazy but I have always wanted to open my own little café," she confided in him.

"I don't think it sounds crazy at all. I've always told you how much I enjoyed your cooking. Just look at mine and Jester's bellies. As they say, the proof is in the pudding," Bubba committed holding his stomach.

"I hate to be the one to tell you Bubba, but we live in a one-horse town. We already have two cafes, not counting the Dixie Dog. Another one would never make it," she said, pointing out the obvious.

"Who says you have to open a restaurant here," Bubba countered.

She looked at him and said in a shocked voice, "What do you mean, leave? Bubba I can't leave; everyone I love lives here," Sherry protested.

"Sherry, I'd bet the farm that your daddy is half way to Lubbock to look at new motor homes. He'd be a damn fool not to be. This town did him shitty, why would he stay here? He worked all his life, he is owed a little fun," Bubba pointed out.

Sherry agreed with his assessment of her father's future. "But what about you? You are here. You and Jester would go to hell in a hand basket if I up and moved off," Sherry argued.

"Well, I don't doubt that for a minute but who says I want to stay here anymore than your father?" he said, surprising her.

She was dumbfounded to say the least. Those words were the last she thought she would ever hear coming from him. Ever since Bubba Lee was old enough to hold down a job, he had one goal: figure out how to buy the ranch back. It was the reason he went to the oil patch at age sixteen, the reason for the year spent on the rodeo circuit and why he did two tours in Vietnam. She always figured if you took that dream away from him, you'd just as soon take away his reason for living.

"What about the ranch Bubba Lee? That's all I have heard about for damn near thirty years. It's your dream, Bubba," she questioned as though it was set in stone.

"Sherry we both know that's never going to happen. Jester would win the White House before the McBride name is once again hanging on the main gate. To be real honest, I gave up on that pipedream a long time ago," he said.

Then, after a pause, he began to grin from ear to ear. "Bubba's got a brand new dream, baby sister," he said with a laugh and then began to tell her about the dream he had a year earlier and how it had stuck with him. He agreed that it sounded crazy, but he couldn't get what he called the "Wild bull dream" out of his head. "And it's all your fault," he said.

"How's it my fault?" she wanted to know.

"Do you remember that book by Jimmy Buffett you bought me last year for my birthday? I know as sure as I'm sitting here, it's what prompted the dream," he said, trying his best to explain.

"I read that book. Are you talking about that story about the Wyoming cowboy?" Sherry asked.

"Tully Mars and Mr. Twain? Yes I am," He answered.

"What exactly are you trying to say; you want to go South?" she asked, trying to follow along.

"Nope, further! I was thinking about some small island in the Caribbean," Bubba told her.

"And do what? Work on our tans? I love you Bubba, but I have no desire to see you in a thong. I'm all for a vacation, but to move to the islands, come on Bubba" she stated.

"No just hear me out, Sherry. I'll bet you there's not a café anywhere on the island chain that serves up good, home-style, Texas cooking. If there is, you can bet your backside it ain't as good as your cooking. Just think about it Sherry, it could be a gold mine," Bubba reasoned.

"And what are you and Jester going to do, wash dishes?" She mused.

Bubba began to laugh. "Hell no, or at least I ain't. Now you might get Jester to lick a plate or two. I'm damn lucky if I wash my own. Believe it or not, I have my own dream job and it has nothing to do with cows or horses. I paid my dues to the saddle," Bubba said in a matter-of-fact way.

"What would that dream occupation be and why haven't I heard you talk about it before this?" Sherry asked curiously.

"I would like to open up a small fishing charter service. You know - take rich people fishing and get paid for it. I've played around with the idea for awhile. I guess I never told you about it because I really wasn't serious about it until now; that and I

24

didn't want you thinking I was nuts," Bubba explained.

"How do you propose we open these ventures; with our looks?" was the next logical question.

"No, although you could pull it off. I, on the other hand, couldn't get a toy boat for the bathtub with mine. Sherry, since I stopped drinking, I've put a sizable amount of my income back. What the hell do I spend money on? I don't drink or smoke. It's not like my dance card is full. The ranch pays for nearly everything else. On top of that, I have my GI bill that I never used.

"And you little sister probably got twice as much. Don't take this wrong, but Sherry you're tight as a tick; not to mention what you could get out of this house.

"Sherry, dreams can come true, I am sure of it. I believe the secret is not to wait until you're too old to enjoy them. I know it means taking a hell of a risk, but ain't that what life is all about? I don't want to push you into anything but ask yourself one thing: after everything that happened this morning, do you think you'd ever be happy here again?" He was doing his best imitation of a lawyer's closing argument.

"Damn Bubba Lee, forget that fishing boat. We need to get you on a used car lot somewhere. You want to talk gold mine?" Sherry kidded.

Bubba took a big drink of ice tea when he had finished. It had been many moons since he had strung so many words together. He was not known as a very talkative person by any stretch of the imagination. It might have been the only way Sherry knew how much it meant to him. On the other hand, she had to be realistic. Did Bubba offer a fair argument or was his head in the clouds? A serious look then appeared on her face.

"Bubba, I hope you don't want an answer today. I mean, there's a lot to consider when totally changing every aspect of your life. I hope you can appreciate that," she said easily, hoping not to bust his bubble.

"I agree. I didn't expect ever asking the question when I left the ranch this morning. I sure as hell don't expect an answer," he said in an understanding tone.

They talked a little longer and then had lunch. Jester had barely cleaned his dog bowl when Bubba called him and told Sherry it was time they get back to the ranch. Although Jester did not have the power of speech, his look conveyed a direct message. "Come on boss, can't you see I just ate? A nap Bubba;

that's what we need," the dog seemed to be saying to his owner.

"I won't leave you hanging for long, I promise," Sherry told him, referring to their earlier conversation.

"I won't beat a dead horse to death, so you take your time," he said before he left.

Sherry drove by her parents' house later that afternoon. She was worried about how her father was handling his termination from a position he had held for over thirty years. She was shocked to find no one was home and yet her mother's car was in the driveway. Her first thought was maybe they were having a late lunch or perhaps an early dinner. She then drove by the two cafes in town to see if she could find her father's pick-up; no such luck. Sherry didn't have any idea where they might be so she went back home and hoped they would call.

She got her wish about three hours later. Her father called to invite her over; he had something he wanted to show her.

"Damn Bubba Lee, sometimes I think you have a crystal ball," she told herself after seeing a new motor home parked in front of her parents' house. She then noticed Bubba's truck parked behind the thirty-foot monster. She decided he had been summoned as well. She had to park across the street because the motor home and Bubba's pick-up nearly took up the entire block on her parents' side of the street.

The first thing she noticed walking up was her mother coming out the door with a tray, a pitcher of tea and glasses. Through the windshield of the RV, she saw her father and Bubba. Her father was in the driver's seat and appeared to be showing his guest something. She later would find out he was showing Bubba the master control panel because it was the first thing he showed her.

"They're like two young boys with a new train set," Sherry's mother committed when she saw her daughter.

Taking the tray away from her mother, she laughed and agreed with her. "You all are awfully festive for everything that has happened today," she said.

"Why not baby girl? I've been looking forward to this day for a long time," her father said, as though the weight of the world had been lifted from his shoulders. "Those suckers on the board of directors did me a favor and don't even know it. Let them poor fools sort this mess out; your mother and I are going to the Grand Canyon,"

It was about then that she realized Bubba was right. Times were changing before her very eyes. She could change with them, or get left behind.

Although she didn't tell him until days later, that was the night she chose to take a chance on Bubba's off-the-wall dream.

Everything in Bubba's world seemed to move at break-neck speed after Sherry agreed to go along with his Caribbean adventure. In a matter of days, he liquidated all the junk he had acquired in his lifetime. He called it a "getting-out-of-Dodge sale". It wasn't long before all he had left were a few books, Jester and his duffle bag. It was all his simple life required; he was a firm believer in traveling light.

Sherry, well that was a different story altogether. Bubba found her using the utmost care packing, labeling and then shipping her worldly belongings to a storage facility in Tampa. He couldn't understand why someone would want to start a new life surrounded by the relics of their past life. But he dared not question her actions, even though they confused him.

One of his friends asked him why he never said anything to her.

"I'm not a smart man, but I know enough not to rile her with such questioning of her behavior," Bubba said, doing his best impression of Forest Gump. "I tell her what I'm thinking and it really would be, Run Forest, Run," he added.

Bubba and Jester camped out at the local motel until she had all her ducks in a row, so to speak. He used his time wisely while he cooled his heels in room 17 at the Ace Motel. Bubba spent most of his days on the phone talking with real estate agents and tour guides that were a time zone away. He wanted to be ahead of the curve if the ball ever got rolling

It was a little past dawn that spring morning when Sherry knocked on Bubba's door. He had been up a couple hours watching the morning news on CNN. The maid at the motel was known to drink a bit and get her hours mixed up. Bubba Lee looked at his watch and figured it was a half-drunk Gloria wanting to get her day over with by check-out time. He was surprised to find Sherry, not the maid, at his door.

"Well if we're going, let's go," Sherry said in a matter-of-fact voice.

"Hell it's about time. I've waited a month to hear those words," Bubba confessed.

In no time at all, he had Jester and his duffle bag in the back seat ready to ride. They smiled at one another as she handed him the car keys. A few minutes later, he pulled the car off on the shoulder of the road just outside of town. They got out and took one last look at the only place they had ever called home.

"Any second thoughts?" he asked Sherry.

"Would it do any good," she answered in a playful voice.

"Hell no, not today!" Bubba said getting back in the car.

Bubba, Sherry, and perhaps the largest dog in Texas, drove off into the morning's haze. Left behind them in their wake were decades of memories, most of which were good. Ahead of the two newly self-described adventurers lay the unmade memories of their future.

In between the bathroom breaks, the dog walking, and the "Hey Bubba, let's stop and take a look at that," it took nearly a full week just to get to the Florida Keys. Bubba was beginning to wonder if it wouldn't have been quicker going by horseback, like in his dream. He held his tongue and marveled at the workings of the female mind, which seemed to run in reverse of his own.

He knew in his heart that once they arrived, it was well worth the wait. Gazing out at the sand bars, reefs, and the cobalt blue Atlantic Ocean made it pretty much self-explanatory. Bubba thought he would have to have an entire week just to take it all in. It was just his luck when he found something he wanted to see, Sherry was ready to get down to brass tacks.

"Oh well," he thought to himself, "I'll have the rest of my life to take it in," he continued.

The next two weeks were spent island hopping. Their quest was three-fold; find a place in the island chain where they both felt comfortable. Once they had accomplished the first goal, the next task was to find the right spot for Sherry to open her small café. Last, but not least, was Bubba finding his boat. The third task is what brought Bubba and Jester to the docks that morning.

They found the perfect little island: not too small and not too big. The people were as friendly as any ever found in Texas. The tourist trade wasn't completely overwhelming, but it was enough to make a good living. The view from the harbor was simply breathtaking.

The best part of the island was the four hundred-year-old town of roughly six-thousand. While there were a few small villages on the island, the town of Saint Rene was by far the most populated. It was on Saint Rene's quaint, cobble stone streets where Sherry found the perfect location for her eatery.

Her lifelong friend, Bubba, was shocked to find her choice was in such a bad state of disrepair. He expected her to settle on a turnkey operation; one ready to start serving food, even before the ink was dry on the contract. Later he would find out that she fell in love with the history of the building before she ever visited the site.

The cut-stone structure was completed in 1836, the same year Texas won her independence from Mexico. The man who had commissioned the building of the structure, might have been the first ex-patriot in American history.

General Matthew Litz had served with Andrew Jackson during the War of 1812. He had been raised by a Cherokee Indian chief after his parents were killed by members of the Creek Nation. Litz would have been content to remain in the army if not for the Indian Removal Act pushed by his former commanding officer and friend. It was as though Jackson was twisting a knife in his back. Litz resigned his commission, wrote a less-than-flattering letter to President Jackson and swore off his American citizenship.

The old general moved to the island and built what would become The Litz Rum Distillery in the very same building that Sherry had just bought. In some ways, she said she could relate to the old general.

In its hundred-and-sixty-year history, the building on the cobblestone street had served many functions. It was a black-powder warehouse in the 1870's, a dry goods store after that, and recently it had been a flower shop. Combined with the latter and the year it was built, Sherry christened it "The Yellow Rose."

Bubba Lee had been shanghaied shortly after the deed to the building was signed. It seemed as though she thought Bubba was a master of all trades. He was a damn good cowboy, some would argue an even better soldier but he was no carpenter. Finally after two weeks of not meeting her expectations, he hired some real carpenters that actually knew what they were doing.

He was waiting on the boardwalk earlier that morning with his duffle bag in hand.

"Going somewhere, Bubba?' she asked when she arrived.

"I got a lead on a boat. I think me and Jester will go have a look see," he informed her.

It wasn't hard to see the disappointment in her eyes. He had hoped to avoid it altogether; about all he could do was head it off.

"Don't worry girl, I hired you some men that know what the hell they're doing. I spend most of my time trying to fix my mistakes. I know you would like you to open the joint before you retire," he said, trying to end with some slight humor.

After she gave it some thought, Sherry knew he was right. She was building her dream; it was time Bubba began work on his.

Her look of disappointment turned into a slight smile. "So where did you find a boat?" she wanted to know.

"The Yucatan, in Mexico," he answered.

"I know where the Yucatan is Bubba Lee, I did go to college," she said lovingly, jerking his chain.

"I've got to meet a seaplane at the dock in about a half hour. I just don't want to leave here with you pissed off at me," he told Sherry.

"No Bubba, you're right! You go find your boat Captain Cowboy. I'll be here and I'll be your harbor. You run along now," she said in a motherly voice as she hugged his neck. In short, that is how Bubba found himself on the dock, awaiting his flight. More importantly, it's how a West Texas cowboy got to the island.

THIRD COAST

Chapter 2

It is said on the bayou that a coon-ass with a high IQ is a mighty dangerous animal. Captain Brian Boulet was such a coon-ass. But dangerous to whom seemed to be the question. He spent his younger years trying to answer. It was a toss-up between society or himself.

Born the only son of a Lake Charles judge, the younger Boulet grew up in a world of privilege. Later in life he would come to the conclusion the term "privilege" was a nice way of saying spoiled.

It was almost that same time when he learned the true nature of the family's wealth. The Boulets obtained their fortune the old fashioned way: they stole it. Boulet wasn't even their real name. Up until the turn of the 20th century, they were the Laffites, with linage going all the way back to the famous privateer Jean Laffite.

Jackson (Laffite) Boulet, Brian's grandfather, might have changed their sir name but not the family's fortune. The old man was losing his faculties when he let the secret slip in the presence of his ten-year-old grandson, thus setting in motion the life of one Captain Boulet.

The younger Boulet was born to be a man of the sea, like his forefathers. The problem was it took thirty some-odd years and three coasts to figure that out.

Brian Boulet, unlike the two generations that preceded him, embraced his family's renegade roots but no more so than when it was time for him to go to college. His father had hoped he would attend LSU and eventually go on to law school, but the young man had other ideas.

His thinking was more on the lines of the University of California at Berkeley. His desired area of study was philosophy. Berkeley made perfect sense to the young man because it had been named after George Berkeley, a noted Irish philosopher of the seventeen hundreds.

The elder Boulet had no idea what a degree in philosophy might net the lad but he couldn't say no to his only son. So in 1958, Judge Boulet put his only son on a plane headed west, hoping for the best.

Brian was held hostage in the great lecture halls of higher education. His captors were the immortal philosophers of past ages: Aristotle, St. Anselm,

David Hume, and other giants of their times in the field of philosophy. Those were the voices that spoke to him.

The great men of other eras lead their young student through subject matters that had always confused man. Topics like free will, religious beliefs, values and the perceptions of the material world were the basic concepts Brian grew to know as the building blocks of knowledge.

While not yet feeling like he had completely mastered the discipline, he graduated at the head of his class in 1962. It was that feeling that drove him into graduate school. By the time 1965 arrived, he felt as though he was the master of all things in the field of philosophy.

The arrogance of possessing such worldly insight and knowing what to do with his unique knowledge seemed to be in conflict. The world was not looking for the next Plato! His options seemed to be few: hide out a few more years in academia striving for a PHD or go back home and clerk for his aging father. Neither option offered that much appeal to Boulet.

He considered both paths as he sipped his coffee in the courtyard of one of the many cafes that dotted the streets of Berkeley. The times were changing all around him as the history of the sixties began to write itself. It began with the Civil Rights Movement and morphed into the anti-Vietnam war revolt.

Movement after movement all but passed him by as he studied for one exam and then the next. Boulet became a little more interested after completing his thesis. He began to dissect the social phenomena from a distance at first. Like a classroom project, he began to apply philosophical theories in a scientific manner.

One night a date took the young philosopher across the Golden Gate Bridge into San Francisco. They ate an early dinner in Chinatown and then went to a poetry reading at a coffee house in the Haight-Ashbury district.

The words touched Boulet in a way he never thought it would. The concepts the poet spoke of were profound and directly related to the times he lived in. He felt a little like Alexander the Great after hearing Aristotle speak for the first time.

Brian and his date joined the poet at his flat after the reading, along with some other couples His date gave him a deep kiss in the middle of evening and in the process, she placed a substance under his tongue.

His mind became charged with a multitude of colors within a matter of minutes. The abstraction of philosophy became tangible as his thoughts obtained form. The acid-laced kiss had a transforming effect over him and affected every aspect of his being. His mind was opened and the cosmos filled it with an almost biblical insight. The world, like a package, seemed to open up but only to him.

While Brian Boulet experienced the almost out-of-body effect, all who attended that night saw the metamorphosis of the once long-time college student. Even his speech changed as he combined a French Creole dialect with the teachings of the great philosophers. Every now and then, he would throw in a little Bugs Bunny for good measure. He didn't care; he was just enjoying the trip.

A few weeks later, Boulet began to make the transition from college graduate to a leader of the counter-culture movement. He had missed out on the other such movements so he was bound and determined not to miss the next one.

He moved to San Francisco with the girl who had taken him to the poetry reading, grew his hair long and began to experiment with several mind-altering chemicals. High on hashish, he began to write his manifesto.

Boulet considered his formal education to be the seeds, and the drugs he was expanding his mind with, the water. Together they would create what many would come to know as the Cajun Seer, the high priest of the gifted.

People began to hear of the man who spoke coon-ass philosophy on the streets of the Bay City and flocked to listen to his psychedelic words of wisdom. Brian Boulet preached of a place where they all could go, a place void of the ills of the world where only peace and love flourished. He called this place Shangri-la, after the fictional valley in James Hilton's book "Lost Horizon".

His following grew and his followers showered him with gifts of sex, money and, yes, drugs. Icons of the day sought an audience with the modern-day philosopher. To the young people, Boulet represented what their leaders could be. To the leaders of the day, men like the coon-ass philosopher represented a threat. Due to his constant use of chemicals, the man himself had no idea what the hell he represented.

A decade of peace and love proved to be anything but. Young men died by the hundreds in a war half a world away. Those who were lucky enough to come back home, came home broken. Two of America's great leaders: Martin Luther King Jr. and

Robert F. Kennedy were gunned down by deranged individuals. Free love was merely the residue in some spaced-out hippy's hashish pipe.

In 1968 Boulet took his first shot of China-white (heroin) and fell madly in love with the illegal drug. Shortly thereafter, he became lost to the world, his followers and most of all himself. The child of wealth, the college graduate, the Seer and been reduced to a skid-row junkie within a year's time.

It was at that point when young Brian's life became a vicious cycle. He spent every waking hour chasing the horse, (heroin) just to feed the monkey (addiction). The boy who had grown up in a plantation-style mansion, spent most nights in a flophouse or if the money was right, a shooting gallery.

The high that he had experienced that first night after the poetry reading was gone. An everyday existence in a living hell had taken its place. The only time he felt halfway comfortable in his skin was on those occasions he visited the wharf. Something about the sea brought a calming effect over him. It had always been that way, even when he was a kid on the Gulf.

Brian Boulet wasn't the only cult leader or icon of his day to come up on the losing end of addiction. It was a sad story that kept repeating itself over and over again. Many, like those soldiers in the Vietnam War, never made it out alive.

It was the overdose death of a virtuoso guitar player that got Boulet to see his world in a new light. He had just seen the young musician three days earlier; they had burned a joint together. He knew deep down that if he stayed in San Francisco. he would be the stiff in the obituaries. The day he left California he vowed to change his life.

His father, Judge Boulet, owned a hunting cabin a half an hour outside of Livingston, Montana. It seemed like the ideal place to shake his way out of the withdrawals he knew were sure to come. What trouble could he get into in the Great Northwest? After all, there were more people at a Grateful Dead Concert than in the whole state of Montana.

Everything went just as Boulet had planned, at least in the beginning. It took about a month for him to get most of his health back. The fresh Montana air seemed to work wonders. It wasn't long before he was chopping his own firewood and working around the place. Manual labor was the one thing he had never tried; it felt good to be self-reliant.

He did his best to shy away from people as much as possible. He only went into town when he absolutely had to. He didn't trust himself around the general public. He didn't realize how taxing the life of the coon-ass Seer had been until his mind had cleared and he had been away from it awhile. In short, he had all the attention he wanted for a while.

Winter came and went. He had read every book in the cabin. His only visitor was his father who had flown up during elk season. It was the first time they had seen one another in a number of years. He didn't know how much he missed philosophical conversations until the week after the judge had gone back to Lake Charles.

Brian was a little steer crazy by the time spring came around. The idea was to go into town, get supplies, have a beer and maybe get laid if he was lucky. Sex was about the only thing he missed from his crash-pad days. In that respect, he was very much a red-blooded American male.

Everything was going to plan until later that afternoon at the bar. He was on his second brew, chatting with a coed from Bozeman. He was doing his best to dazzle her with his philosophical line of bullshit when six or seven men came in dressed like cowboys. He figured they were just some hands from a nearby ranch.

"Hey Brian, Brian Boulet! I'll be damned, is that really you?" a man yelled over the jukebox.

Boulet looked confused, trying his best to place the man. The stranger got a beer and then invited himself to sit down with the slightly dazed Brian.

"You don't remember me, do you? Well no one could really blame you; that was one hell of a night we had in San Fran a few years back," the man said, trying to jar Boulet's memory.

There were so many nights in San Francisco he didn't remember; how could he remember the exact one the man was referring to. He figured if he played along with the man it might come to him. It never did but that was beside the point.

The man's name L. J. Pete and he was from Los Angeles. He was a grip in Livingston working on a movie called "El Rancho Deluxe." The men with him were not cowboys at all, just a few others working on the set.

A funny thing happened that night. While Boulet was trying to get caught up and figure out where he knew Pete from, one of those movie types moved in and stole the coed he was with. He was about to get pissed when Pete said he had just gotten some smack (heroin) in from the Coast. He figured "what the hell would it hurt," so the two men went back to the grip's room to shoot up.

It was his first shot of dope in ten months. Damn, the sex he could have been having that night couldn't have been that good. But a night spent in a drug-manufactured Nirvana came with a high price tag. Before Brian knew what hit him, he was chasing the elusive horse once again.

Boulet's second winter in Montana was as different as day and night. It might have been the coldest he had ever been. He didn't care too much about reading, chopping wood or the great outdoors. The next fix and where he was going to get it was all he concerned himself with.

Through a friend of a friend, he found a connection on the reservation. Robert Grey-Fox was a Vietnam vet who rotated back to the reservation with a nasty habit. With no means of visible support, he began to trade in Mexican Black Tar Heroin. His best customer was a spaced-out coon-ass named Brian Boulet.

Boulet didn't know his connection was leading a double life. The majority of the money Gray-Fox was making off the drugs he was using to buy fire arms for the N.A.B. (Native American Brotherhood). The N.A.B. was a splinter group of the faction who held hostages at the sight of Wounded Knee.

Boulet was in the middle of a good drug binge when he noticed a black car following him. He wasn't really sure of anything. He had been speed balling (shooting heroin and cocaine) so it could have been the paranoia from the coke.

Four days into a damn good dope run, his paranoia picked his ass up and threw him in the back seat of the black car. His illusions in reality had badges that read the three letters every doper hates to hear: FBI.

They took him into the mountains where they questioned him for several hours. They wanted to know what his involvement was in the movement and when and where they were planning to attack.

"I'm a junky damn it. Do I look like I could over-throw anything? You boys are pretty desperate if I am all you can come up with." They roughed him up pretty good for his last remark.

 The federal agents left him in the woods shaking from the lack of a fix and bleeding from their attitude adjustment. All he could do was hurt and think about the situation he found himself in. He had left the West Coast because the counter-cultural movement damn near killed him. Suddenly he found himself in another movement and although he had no part in it, it was still trying to kill him. He was in bad need of an exit sign. As soon as he could muster up the strength to walk out of where had been dumped, he was out of there.

A day later, Boulet had came up with enough smack to get him wherever he was going. With everything he owned in the back seat of a car his father had bought him, he left Livingston, Montana, bound for who knows where.

He stopped at a little bar south of Billings to fix up and have a beer. He was seated at the bar nodding in and out when he heard the sweetest sound: steel drums with a Caribbean flavor. He didn't know if it was his mind telling him to go somewhere warmer or Bob Marley on the juke box.

He convinced himself it was a combination of the two and pointed his car toward Florida. Three days later, he was sitting in the sunshine of Miami Beach looking out over the blue Atlantic Ocean.

It didn't take long for Boulet to establish himself. He had always had a way of fitting in wherever he went. With his above-average intellect and a gift for gab, he had a way of making himself the center of attention. But, like always, and almost on cue, he fell in with the wrong crowd.

The Costa-Tines were a gang of Cuban refugees loosely held together by blood and more by profits. Most, but not all of them, left mother Cuba with their parents after Castro rose to power. Their parents held high positions in the government and were put there by the American mob to oversee their gambling interests. They would have been marked for death if they stayed in their homeland.

The Americanized generation of the Cuban refugees had turned to smuggling drugs from South America: bundles of weed, Peruvian flack and heroin, depending what was in vogue at the time. The Cubans were efficient in their pursuit of the drug trade. Each faction of Costa-Tines was charged with a different responsibility of the business.

Pepi, the oldest of the blood cousins, had a fleet of large, modified boats used to transport the contraband from the drop site to the shore. Leon and his crew ran the product from Key Largo up to Miami. Martin and his two younger siblings were in charge of distribution. The whole operation ran just as smooth as any Fortune 500 company.

Boulet met Pepi in a bar in the Keys late one night. He was there hoping to score because his stash was running thin. The smuggler had a reason for being at Sloppy Joe's that night. He was waiting on a phone call about a shipment. The first rule of drug smuggling: take it as a given the Feds have your private phone tapped.

"You know whose barstool you are sitting on, friend?" Pepi asked, trying to strike up a friendly conversation as he waited for his call.

"No sir, if it's yours I'll move," Boulet answered nervously. A day without a fix was beginning to wear on him.

"No amigo you're fine. I was just going to point out that is where Ernest Hemingway, the classic American writer always sat," Pepi explained.

"No shit, the same writer who penned, "The Old Man and the Sea?" Brian Boulet marveled.

"That's one of my favorite books. My grandfather was a fisherman from Cuba. The story somehow always reminded me of him," the smuggler shared.

The conversation seemed to come easy after the first few exchanges between them. Both men knew the other was hiding something but it didn't seem to matter. They were just two men sharing a beer while they waited for time to pass; each for different reasons.

An hour passed before the bartender told Pepi he had a call. Any other night the smuggler would have just left anyone he was talking to at the bar, but he had a gut feeling about Boulet.

"I have to go take care of a little business. Would you like to come along?" Pepi asked

Boulet had that lost look about him, the same look Pepi used to see in his younger brother's eyes. The look conveyed both an uncertainty and certainty. Boulet wanted to go but there was that little thing about the monkey on his back.

"I see you have a need. Let me take this call and then we'll fix you up," the man said in an almost whisper.

Boulet never understood why he left the bar with a man he had barely known for an hour. Perhaps it was for the promise of a fix, or maybe it went deeper than that. Kindred spirits are often found in the least likely of places.

Pepi made a stop on the way to the port where he conducted his business affairs. The house was dark, all but a single light in the front room. A pit bull began to bark from the porch.

"Hush Mongo, you'll wake the dead," Pepi told the dog.

Boulet didn't know where he was, but he had been to a thousand such places on his road to hell. The only difference was the breed and the name of the dog. People come and go to such houses, all hours of the day and night. They are all lost souls with a single thought in mind: feed the freaking hole in their arm.

Pepi was back in a matter a minutes. "Will this make the night pass easier?" he asked, handing the packet of heroin to his new friend.

Boulet didn't have to thank the man, his eyes told Pepi all he needed to know. It didn't take that long to get to the slips where the smuggler kept his boats.

"You can you use the office to fix up and then we'll go on a little boat ride if you are up to it," Pepi told Brian in a kind voice.

With the offer of the deep-sea adventure still hanging in the air, Boulet put the dope in his pocket, thinking, "I guess I'll do it later."

The small act from a self-confirmed junky told Pepi a lot about the man. It would be one of the building blocks to their friendship. It would also awaken a love for the sea which Boulet was totally unaware of.

Pepi had three forty-five-foot boats lined up in their slips. Each was just as beautiful as the next. It wasn't hard to see they had been built by master craftsmen at least a half a century earlier. The boats would have been considered fine yachts in their heyday. The lines of these crafts would have made even the late Kennedy brothers envious.

Pepi waited until his new friend was aboard the Isabel before he untied her from her slip. He then went to her helm and turned the ignition switch to the Cummins Diesel in the belly of the boat. Boulet looked surprised as a puff of black smoke seemed to awaken the slumbering Isabel.

"I thought this type of craft was built for sailing," Boulet committed, trying to seem knowledgeable.

"She was a maiden of the wind a lifetime ago, but times and needs change," Pepi said over the hum of the engine. "She was modified to meet my purpose, just as the others have been. But make no mistake about it, she's just as graceful under sail as she ever was."

Boulet knew better than to ask what his purpose for the Isabel might be. A man who could score a balloon of smack at the drop of a hat, one didn't question. The graveyard was full of fools who asked too many stupid questions. Boulet had no intention of joining them. The Grim Reaper would come for him soon enough.

A haunting feeling came over the one-time leader of a forgotten movement. The wind that blew through his hair as the boat made her way to sea, felt like the frigid fingers of the past. The only question was, "Whose past?"

The addict in him was beginning to reconsider rather or not he should have fixed up before leaving the shore. He had heard and seen many things when addicts were coming off the horse "heroin." Withdrawal was one hell of a bitch to ride. "They had never reached out so early before, but what else could it be," he asked himself.

It was at that point he heard a voice, "One more coast," it called to him.

He was startled at first, but then the voice seemed to bring a sense of calm to his being. He began to ride the waves like only a true seaman could. His host marveled at the way Boulet took to the open water.

Thirty miles out, a seaplane waited with her illegal cargo. A signal flashed between the two crafts and then men appeared at the plane's door. Pepi maneuvered the Isabel closer and closer once he saw the coast was clear.

The men on the plane started handing bundles to Pepi out the cargo door. In turn, Pepi would hand them off to Boulet to be stowed below. He took to the task without any questions. None were needed; it didn't take a whole lot of calculations to realize he had stumbled onto a smuggling operation.

That night set the wheels in motion for the next year of Brian Boulet's life. He later told an out-of-place cowboy that it was during that year he learned his ancient family's business from the ground up.

The Isabel was his classroom and Pepi his teacher for the next three months. He would learn to read charts by day and at night he would learn to sail by the stars. In the middle of his nautical education, he also learned the life of a drug trafficker.

It was the thrill of the life. While not curbing his addiction, it seemed to stop the downward spiral. Boulet became what the drug cultural would refer to as a chipper (using just enough of a particular drug, not to get high but to stave off the withdrawal that comes with addiction).

It was only after Pepi deemed his student both trust-worthy and sea-worthy that he granted permission for Boulet's first solo run. He was confident, and yet a little nervous, as he pointed the Isabel out to sea. He took to his station at the wheel as though he was born to it. From then on, once or twice a week, it was Captain Boulet and the Isabel making their midnight runs.

The smuggling life proved to be good to Boulet. It wasn't long before he had a condo overlooking the Keys, a ten-year-old Jag, and a stable of girlfriends, all drug users, of course, that he called his "girl-fiends." Life was good for the Lake Charles coon-ass as the Age of Aquarius came to an end.

It was misting that night Pepi told his young Captain to meet him at Sloppy Joe's. Something in the old smuggler's voice told Boulet his friend was worried. He listened carefully while the man voiced his concerns.

"The Feds are on to us; we're gonna have to move our pick-up point further out. We need to add a couple barrels of extra fuel. You handle it and I'll meet you at the boat with the latitudes and longitudes," Pepi said, instructing his partner in crime.

Two hours passed before the normally calm Pepi arrived. Boulet noticed that night his friend was anything but calm. He began to have a bad feeling and wished Pepi would call the whole thing off. He even suggested as much but Pepi told him the bird was all ready in the air. It made him feel a little better when Pepi decided to go with him. It had been awhile since they made a run together.

Two hours passed before the mist stopped falling and by then they were twice as far out as they normally were.

"Any further my friend, and we'll be in your family's homeland," Boulet said, trying to lighten up an already dreary night. "We won't have to worry about the Feds, 'cause we'll be in Fidel's sights."

Pepi forced a smile about the time the first signal appeared from the aircraft. "Good, the sooner we get this shit loaded and on our way, the better I'll feel," the smuggler confided in Boulet.

Boulet brought the helm about until the Isabel was port side of the sea plane. The cargo door flew open and two men of Spanish decent began unloading their booty. Search lights from the other side of the plane suddenly turned night into day.

"This is the United States Coast Guard. Be prepared to be boarded," came a loud voice over a speaker.

A smuggler's nightmare was unfolding before Boulet's eyes. Just about the time he thought it couldn't get any worse, one of the men on the plane opened up with a Mac Ten assault weapon. The damn fool was shooting nine mm bullets while the other side had a fifty caliber. The only good thing about the mess Boulet found himself in was the seaplane was between the Coast Guard cutter and the Isabel.

He knew he had to do something quick. Bullets were ripping through the plane's fuselage and flying all around. All he could think of was getting the hell out of the line of fire as fast as he could.

He ran to the bridge and pushed the throttle all the way down. Black smoke began to pour from the Isabel's exhaust. The old girl lunged forward in the water. Gunfire began to fade in the distance. Boulet knew it was only a matter of time before the gun battle with the plane was over and the Coast Guard would be on his ass.

He had a choice to make: keep running or stop long enough to throw the dope overboard. He knew the decision wasn't his alone to make, but where the hell was Pepi? He called out to his friend as he throttled Isabel's engine back. No reply came from the Cuban smuggler.

"Damn, tell me you didn't fall overboard," Boulet said, half heartedly joking as he made his way to the back of the boat.

He found his friend face up on the deck. Pepi's eyes stared lifelessly up at the heavens. Boulet almost threw-up when he saw what destructive carnage a fifty caliber bullet could reap on the human body. He didn't need to check for a pulse to know the old smuggler was gone. He gleaned that much from the seven-inch hole in Pepi's chest.

The death of his boss created a whole new set of problems for Boulet. He would never draw another breath as a free man if he was caught with the drugs and the body. The dope and the smuggler both had to be buried at sea.

He said a quick prayer for the dead and then released the body over the side. He felt sad that he could do no more for the man who had trusted him. However, Boulet knew if the roles were reversed; if it was him lying dead in a pool of blood, Pepi would not hesitate to chunk his Cajan ass over the rail.

Pepi's body was only half of what needed to go overboard. Just when Boulet thought it couldn't get any worse, it did. It turned out those fifty caliber shells could do about the same to a boat's hull as it could do to a human body. He found two holes in the side of the Isabel when he went below to retrieve the dope.

One was above the waterline and didn't pose much of a threat unless he ran into the high seas. He wasn't so lucky with the second threat; the boat was taking on water at a rapid rate. Without thinking and relying on his training, he fired up the pumps to push the water out. He then plugged the hole as best he could.

Boulet then set out doing what he had come below to do: taking his illegal cargo top-side and disposing of it. He shut down the engine and all the lights. He knew if he wanted to survive the night, he had to become invisible.

Boulet was at the end of his rope and in need of a fix. He was so concerned with not getting caught that he hadn't thought to save some of his snow-white cargo for himself. He knew for all purposes of that night, he was screwed nine ways to Sunday. Perhaps the hand of fate took pity on the man or the Lord saw something worth saving. A thick fog began to settle around the Isabel, hiding her from the evils of the night.

Morning brought a whole new set of issues for Boulet to try to get his head around. It would be a major feat, considering he felt the onset of withdrawal. First his nose began to run and then the sweats; soon would come the shakes. All the classic symptoms of addiction would visit him just like the ghosts did Scrooge in the Charles Dickens story.

It would be tough but nothing he hadn't gone through before. Withdrawals were the known, what really preyed on his nerves was the unknown. He had no idea if he was a fugitive or not, so he couldn't go back.

Even if the authorities weren't looking for him, if he showed up in the Keys with no dope and no Pepi, the cartel would be. It was the quickest way he knew to become gator bait in the Glades. All he could think to do was point the Isabel west and travel deeper into the Gulf of Mexico.

Captain Brian Boulet was a man in need of a miracle, but before it came, he would have to endure a little hell. The boat was taking on water about as fast as he was running out of fuel. It would not be long before he had to put her under sail. He just prayed the pumps would hold out long enough to reach a friendly shore.

The third night alone on the Isabel proved to be the longest. He had been some fifty hours without a fix. That was something every hard-core addict calculated right down to the second. A storm was starting to brew up in the East; about all he could do was try to outrun it. Being under sail and taking on water made that pretty much an impossibility.

The wind picked up to thirty knots as the rain began to fall. Like his withdrawal from the poison he had been injecting, he'd have to ride the storm out. Lightning began to hit all around him as he clung to what little hope he had left.

Suddenly with a flash of a lightning bolt, he swore he saw the face of Jesus Christ. It humbled him to the point that he fell to his knees. As he was looking skyward, the Isabel's mask formed a perfect cross.

Once again he heard the voice he'd heard a year earlier, "One more coast." Just like the first time, he had no idea what was intended, but it gave him comfort. He swore to himself that if he made it out of this mess alive, he'd never stick another spike in his arm.

The next morning he got his chance. He had drifted off to sleep some time during the early morning hours and the sound of a tug boat in the channel rousted him from his rack. He could hardly believe his eyes on what was before him. Was it dry land or heaven? Either way, he didn't care. What looked to be heaven at first glance was, in reality, Port Bolivar on the Texas coast.

A month later, after borrowing the money from his father to fix the Isabel's hull, Captain Boulet sailed out of the harbor heading south. He was clean and sober for the first time in what seemed to be a lifetime. In his wake was his past. He never would see America again, a price he'd have to pay for his youth run aground. Ahead of him lay a calm sea; he hoped it was a sign of things to come. Beneath his feet was the deck of the one-time Isabel. She had been newly christened The Third Coast. "It took the West Coast, East Coast, and the Gulf Coast to turn my life around," he told his father after he asked about the strange name. The Coast of Texas was his one more coast.

THERE'S A COWBOY IN THE JUNGLE

Chapter 3

The Yucatan Peninsula jets out northeastward from Mexico. On the eastern side of the peninsula lie the blue waters of the Caribbean Sea. The western side includes the rich fishing waters of the Gulf of Mexico. The Yucatan is rich in both history and culture. Cortez was the first documented European to reach her shores in the 16th century. The ancient, advanced civilization of the Mayans is still evident in the stone ruins they left behind.

Cortez was not the last seaman to be captured by the beauty of the Yucatan. Many a sea-faring man has found comfort in the inviting surf of The Bay of Campeche. So Bubba Lee's thoughts were not unique to him as the seaplane touched down in her waters.

A three-hour ride from his new island home to the Yucatan left nothing to do but talk to his pilot. Jim Moore was the seasoned airman who had picked the West Texas cowboy and his massive pooch up earlier in the day. Conversation went along the usual male lines once the man got past Bubba's four-legged traveling companion.

One of the topics the two men covered was sports. Bubba was a died-in-the-wool Dallas Cowboy fan. The pilot's favorite NFL team was the New Orleans Saints. One team had multiple championships while the other barely had multiple wins. Needless to say, the conversation was short and left some two-and-a-half hours of empty space to be filled.

Next on the docket for discussion were the movies. It was a pretty good bet, from the way Bubba Lee was dressed, that Westerns would be in his well house.

"You ever read a book called, "Lonesome Dove?" the pilot asked his passenger.

"Isn't that one of Larry McMurtry's books?" Bubba answered. "I never read that one but I've read "Leaving Cheyenne." It was a damn good read."

"About a month ago, I flew a camera crew out to your neck of the woods to start to shoot the film, based on the book," Moore reported.

"No shit!" Bubba said referring to the first McMurtry stories to be transferred to the Big Screen. "If it's anything like "Hud," it ought to be a damn good flick. In my opinion, Paul Newman is the best actor there ever was," Bubba continued, remembering the actor who had the lead.

"Brother we might not agree on football, but I am right there with you when it comes to Newman," Moore said. "Did you catch "Butch Cassidy and the Sundance Kid? Now there was a movie."

The topic of Paul Newman's greatest movies would occupy the next hour of the flight. From *The Left Handed Gun* to *The Hustler* and then Tennessee Williams' *Cat on a Hot Tin Roof*, the conversation went from scene to scene, then line to line. The men went through the complete catalog of Newman's movies from the 1950s and '60s.

Moore made it a practice not to pry into the affairs of his customers. Some people came from America on vacations, while others had shady business arrangements. Moore thought it best to run a "no questions asked" charter service. However, that day, after reviewing the last of the Paul Newman pictures, the man decided to break his own company policy.

"What takes you to the Yucatan: business or pleasure?" the pilot asked.

"Well sire, a little of both," Bubba answered and then began to tell his new friend about the "wild bull" dream and how it convinced him to pull up stakes and move to the islands.

For the past month, Bubba had no one but Sherry to talk to, so with Moore he became a regular chatterbox. Later he guessed his words were just fighting to get out. Bubba began to tell the man about his plan to buy a boat and run a little fishing service. He said the pursuit of a boat was what his reason was for visiting the Yucatan. He added that he always wanted to see that section of Mexico. He then said he and old Jester were going to be the first man-and-dog fishing crew in the island chain.

Bubba Lee saved the best part of his tale for last. He told Moore his dog wasn't the only one he had brought to the tropics with him. His adopted sister, Sherry, had also come to open up a café. "I'll tell you one thing Moore, you ain't ate until you ate Sherry's cooking," the boastful cowboy said. "She knows food the way we know Newman. You're gonna have to come when she gets the joint open. Hell, it will be my treat."

"It's nice to meet some Americans down here not running from something," Moore committed. "We usually get two types of Americano's in the tropics: Those on vacation and those on the run.

"What about you Moore, are you running from anything?" Bubba said joking.

"You're damn right friend, I'm running from the cold. I was a bush pilot for twenty years up in Alaska. You name the pipeline and chances are I flew it. I skimped and saved until I had enough to go south like the rest of the birds," said Moore, beginning to tell a little about himself.

"I guess you are right about the running part," Bubba stated.

"What do you mean?' the pilot wanted to know.

"Today, I am running from my little sister, a hammer and a day's work," Bubba mused. Both men had a good laugh.

"You say you're going to look at a boat? Perhaps I know the party in question and I could help. The tropics are not as big as you might think. For better or worse, everyone practically knows everyone else," Moore said, offering his assistance.

Bubba took a piece a paper out of his shirt pocket, and read aloud, "Captain Boulet."

"Captain Brian Boulet," Moore repeated adding the man's first name.

"I guess so, why?" Bubba Lee asked. "Man Bubba, Captain Boulet, that's one strange duck. I mean I haven't heard anything bad about him; he's just out there, if you know what I mean," Moore was doing his best to describe the Captain but he could tell his passenger wanted to hear more.

"They tell me Boulet sailed into port from out of nowhere about twenty years ago. He's been rumored to be just about anything under the sun, from a genius that cracked up, to the ghost of Captain Morgan, an 18th century pirate," Moore explained.

"Do you know the man, or anything about a boat he might have for sale?" came Bubba's next question.

"I've played chess with the man a time or two, said Moore, trying to describe Boulet. "I can tell you he's educated and refined. He does love to talk about philosophy. I've tried to keep with him, but hell, I'm just an old bush pilot. What the hell do I know about philosophy? He's as gruff as they come. I imagine living in an old Mayan ruin without the comforts of the modern world could make anyone a little gruff.

"The only boat I've ever seen is the Third Coast. She's a pretty thing, I'll tell you that; probably built early in the nineteen-hundreds, back when craftsmanship really counted for something. She's not one of those cookie-cutter, fiberglass numbers that you see these days. This lady has class and a diesel engine to back it up. I'm not an authority on boats but I don't need to be to tell you the Third

Coast is top shelf. It's kind of hard to think Boulet would ever part with the boat, but like I said, he a strange duck," said Moore, finishing up.

"Well that's a lot more than I knew when I left this morning," Bubba said to the pilot. "I just hope this doesn't prove to be wild-goose chase."

"If it makes you feel any better, I'll be around for a few days if you need a ride home," Moore assured Bubba.

"I appreciate that," Bubba said as his pilot taxied the seaplane to the docks.

The wooden planks on the dock led to the ancient cobblestone road in the town of Progreso. Bubba saw a young Indian boy holding a cardboard sign with his last name printed on it waiting by the road.

"I am McBride," he told the boy.

"Good, Captain say bring you pronto," the boy said in broken English.

"Well son, the good Captain is gonna have to wait until I get me and my dog a bite to eat," Bubba told the boy.

A half a block down the road, the boy pointed to a taco stand. Bubba surprised the boy and ordered six tacos in the young man's tongue. All those years being raised by Peto, the old Mexican cook, he could speak better Mexican than the Mexicans. Bubba handed his new guide two tacos, gave Jester two and then ate two himself.

The boy tried to eat but couldn't take his eyes off of Bubba's four-legged friend. It was plain to see he had never seen such a large dog.

"I use him to plow the onion fields," Bubba said, joking with the boy. The boy didn't understand the joke until Bubba told him again in his own language. The boy began to laugh at the gringo's joke.

"We go see the Captain now," the boy repeated his earlier statement.

"Yes, we go see the Captain now," Bubba agreed.

Bubba and Jester followed the boy down an old foot path to the edge of a river. It reminded Bubba of the rivers in Vietnam, not the ones back in Texas. Most of those you could step across the biggest part of the year. Not the one he was looking at. The boy called it, Rio Lagartos. Bubba could tell the river was deep from her banks.

The foot path turned to follow the river. It only took a few steps before the shoreline disappeared from view due to the heavy jungle. It was another attribute reminding him of his time in Southeast Asia.

The river was deep enough and in the jungle's density, Bubba saw how easily one could hide a fairly large boat. He had heard of such inlets; stories were told how pirates used them to escape the crown. He was beginning to wonder if he had made an appointment with a buccaneer of old.

A mile and a half down the path, Bubba came to a clearing in the jungle. In the middle of the clearing, rising up out of the earth was a three-level, ancient Mayan temple. Bubba was amazed how well it was preserved. If he didn't know any better, he would say the builders of the great temple had only recently moved out. The truth was that the Mayan had been gone for centuries. Suddenly he saw something out of the corner of his eye.

"Damn, tell me you're not one of those damn parrot heads looking for Buffett or the keys to Margaritaville," said a voice. "What's the deal with the horse-like dog?"

It was easy to see how one could make that assumption. There stood Bubba wearing his cowboy boots, cowboy hat and a shirt that looked like he had found it in the closet of Thomas Magnum (a character from the TV series "Magnum PI). Years earlier Jimmy Buffett had recorded a song that mirrored Bubba's appearance: *There's a Cowboy in the Jungle* was the name of the ditty.

"No," Bubba said trying to locate the person who belonged to the voice in the brush. "I like Jimmy's songs and his books are wonderful, but I am down here to look at a boat. As far as the second part of your question, this is Jester. He's more than just a dog, he's family" Bubba Lee answered as though no one had ever asked about Jester before.

"Sorry about that, I meant no disrespect to the dog. You'd be surprised how many come looking for Buffett's imaginary port. You must be McBride," said a man coming out of the shadows. "I like a little Buffett too, just don't tell anyone," he said, holding out his hand to shake his visitor's.

Captain Boulet was exactly how Moore had described him. He had long, black-and-silver hair pulled back in a pony tail. A long-sleeve shirt that was unbuttoned all the way, with a pair of tan shorts and flip flops made up the rest of his dress.

"Brian Boulet, at your service," said the Captain. Folks around here call me Captain. I never did figure out why, it seems all one must do is acquire a boat and one becomes a Captain. It doesn't matter if the damn fool can sail it or not. You buy The Third Coast, you'll be a Captain." The old Captain thought a minute, "Captain Cowboy, it has a ring to it," he offered.

"I don't know about that," Bubba objected. "Sounds like a comic-book super hero and I ain't one of those - not by damn sight,"

"Yes indeed, I see your point McBride," Boulet agreed.

Boulet asked how the visitor's trip was and made a little small talk before inviting the Texas cowboy up to the ancient dwelling. Bubba wanted to see the boat but didn't want to seem like an ungrateful guest. So he agreed to follow his host up the mountain of steps.

He was surprised to see how well furnished the old Captain's lair was. A Lazy Boy recliner sat below some well-placed windows. He had read about how advanced the Mayan builders were but he was seeing this first hand. Next to the recliner was shelf after shelf of books older than he was.

He could add up the situation pretty easily. The Mayans had placed the windows in the exact location to capture the most light and Boulet was taking full advantage of it for his reading. "Ingenious," he thought to himself.

He would discover it was classic Boulet. He had his entire living quarters laid out to make use of what the old ones left behind. The cool, dark rooms in the ruins were where Boulet had his food storage and his sleeping quarters. It was as clear as day that the old Captain had mastered living without worldly comforts.

Boulet offered his guest a snack from the freshly picked fruit on the table. His guest picked up a banana and peeled it.

"Nice place you have here," said the Texan, complimenting his host. "Don't know if I have heard of someone doing what you've done but it's clear to see it works."

"Well McBride it wasn't the easiest thing I ever tried to do," said the old Captain. "The Mexican government and a whole gang of the activist threw one hell of a fit. This part of the country has more damn ruins than you can shake a stick at. I mean they have ruins literally on top of ruins. I'll be dead and gone by the time they get around to excavating half of them. They put up a hell of a fight."

"Damn it sounds like you went against some pretty stiff odds. How did you pull it off?" Bubba asked.

"The first thing you must know about this country is that anything or anyone can be bought," said Boulet speaking like he was in a lecture hall. "Since I've been here, I've made a pretty damn good living transporting cargo. The second thing you must know is how to spread it around."

Bubba was smart enough to know not to ask about what sort of cargo the old Captain was transporting. In that part of the world, cargo came in many forms - some even human.

"I suppose you're in a hurry to meet her," Boulet surmised.

"Meet who? Oh! See the boat. That's kinda what I'm here for," Bubba said, trying to not sound like a dumb ass or a smart ass. He figured he failed on both counts after hearing what came out of his mouth. Evidently the Captain either didn't see it the same or he let it slide.

The two men went down the ancient steps they had climbed up thirty minutes earlier. Even if Bubba left the Yucatan without a boat, he could honestly tell Sherry he had one hell of a workout.

"It's a damn shame I tell you, a damn shame," Bubba repeated trying to catch his breath.

"What's a damn shame, McBride?" a confused Boulet asked.

"It's a damn shame them Mayan people, as smart as they were, didn't invent elevators," Bubba answered.

"I thought the same thing the first hundred or so times I went up and down them," Boulet said after he stopped laughing.

The cowboy and the Captain walked side by side down the foot path that led to the cove where Boulet had The Third Coast anchored. The old Captain couldn't remember exactly what he thought the first time he ever laid eyes on her. He hoped it was something like what the cowboy must have been feeling because his face lit up in a glow. It was love at first sight; there was no doubt about it.

"She's swift in the water, under sail or engine driven. She turns a lot quicker and smoother in the water than most of the newer ones," the Captain went on, talking about her attributes. He then noticed the blank look on Bubba's face and the unthinkable dawned on him.

"Have you ever sailed a craft of this size, son?" Boulet asked. Bubba shook his head "no."

"Have you ever sailed any craft before," Boulet asked again. Once again the answer was "no."

"Tell me son, can you swim?" was the Captain's final question. "I can do that," Bubba answered. "Good,'cause I fear if you buy this boat, you'll be doing plenty of that," Boulet said shaking his head.

"You could teach me to sail couldn't you?" pleaded Bubba. "With all due respect, someone taught you. I'd be willing to pay."

"Hell son, where am I going to find the time; I've got a business to run," Boulet told him.

"What business, if I buy the boat?" Bubba pointed out.

The Captain motioned for Bubba to follow him. The next cove was a half a mile away. In her waters there was another boat anchored. The Deliverance was twice the size of her little sister, The Third Coast.

"Damn, she's a beauty," Bubba said scratching his head.

"My old man was a tight old fart," said the Captain. "He saved damn near every nickel he ever made. The old judge died about a year ago. The funny thing was he couldn't take it with him. He thought he passed on his dilemma to me. Not me, I sunk every dime, and more, into her. Now can you understand why I don't have the time to teach you how to sail The third Coast?"

Who knows where Bubba's next idea came from; perhaps it was out of desperation. He threw caution to the wind and went for the whole ball of wax.

"Captain, a ship this size will need to have to a crew, right?" he asked.

"Me and two others," Boulet answered.

Bubba took a big breath, then said, "What if I was one of them. I mean you wouldn't have to pay me a dime; just teach me how to sail. I'll buy The Third Coast and sail her away when you think I'm ready. That's if you haven't already hired a crew."

Boulet liked the Texas cowboy. He had the guts to go after what he wanted and wouldn't take "no" for an answer. He could tell the man that he didn't have the time or the patience to teach seamanship on the fly but he doubted if it would do any good.

"Well no McBride," said the Captain. "I haven't crewed the ship as of yet, I only received ownership of the boat a few days ago. I was just trying to figure out all her nuances for myself when I heard that you were interested in The Third Coast.

"Even if I went along with your proposal, it still leaves me a man down. But I suppose it's better than being two men short," the old Captain reasoned.

Another idea hit Bubba and he blurted out, "Captain, where is the nearest phone? I think I have the perfect man for the job."

"Wait a damn minute McBride, I barely have patience for one newbie, not two," Boulet said objecting.

"Not to worry sir, he's well seasoned, spending most of his life sailing freighters on the Great Lakes,"

Jon Carpenter's mother had a dream that her son would go off to college and be more than his sea-faring father. Her dreams were dashed when her son proved to be as hard-headed as his old man. His decision not to attend the University of Michigan made the young man eligible for the draft.

A month and a half after his eighteenth birthday, Jon Carpenter woke up in the shit: the shit being the GI term for war. He was luckier than most although he didn't realize it at the time. The first Sergeant to the young recruit looked like some dumb-ass hick at best; at worst someone bucking for a section eight, and might get them all killed.

He soon learned not to be so quick to judge, nothing was as it appeared to be in Nam. The first Sergeant, who wore cowboy boots and a hat, proved more than once to be the only one between Carpenter and Arlington National Cemetery.

The cowboy and the Yankee seaman stayed in touch after they rotated back to the world. From time to time, one would visit the other. Carpenter had even worked on the ranch after one of his misguided attempts at romance. It was that Jon Carpenter that Bubba learned to love like a little brother. Jon was in love or in a tavern when he wasn't working on a freighter on the lakes.

Bubba Lee was hoping when he put in the call to the states that he might catch his old friend in between jobs as well as girlfriends. It wasn't that Carpenter's old Sergeant wished him any ill will; it was just the only time he could find him.

Bubba called five known Carpenter haunts before hitting pay dirt: "The Ice House Bar," came a voice on the other end of the line.

"You don't happen to have a cry-in-your-beer, she-did-me-wrong Jon Carpenter in there do you?" Bubba asked the man

"Sure do. You want him," was the man's response.

Bubba had been trying to find his friend for over an hour and was about out of change when he finally got hold of the man.

"This is Carpenter, I don't know how you found me but if I owe you money, you're gonna have to get in line," the half-drunk man said stuttering.

"Stand down soldier! It's me: Bubba," he said, assuring his friend he wasn't a bill collector.

"Damn Bubba, I've been trying to get a hold of you for a week. I called the ranch and some idiot said you moved to the islands. What's up with that? Anyway Sarge, I'm in need of an escape clause if you know what I mean," the man rambled on.

"Well son I have a disappearing act of a lifetime," Bubba told his friend. "Go find yourself a pot of coffee and get your gear. I'll have a ticket waiting for you at the airport."

"Just where am I going?" was the only question Carpenter had.

"Mexico," was his old Sergeant's one-word answer.

Bubba called Sherry after he said his goodbyes to his army buddy. He wanted to let her know his plans had been altered. Evidently his dream was going to be a little harder to obtain than he thought. He then gave her the bad news: he was going to be some time. He would call every chance he could and do his best to try to talk Captain Boulet into stopping by their little island whenever they were in the vicinity.

The part where he told her he might not be home for a few months went better than he thought. He could only guess that her new carpenters were working out well for her. He had hopes his old Carpenter would work out too. She made Bubba promise before they hung up the phone to not miss her grand opening.

"I'll be there, even if I have to swim," he promised before he hung up the phone.

Bubba had agreed to meet the Captain at an eatery in town once he had all his calls made. The idea, Bubba thought, was to have some supper, discuss how he was going to retrieve Carpenter from the airport at Cancun and get to know one another.

He found Jim Moore in a highly contested chess game with the Captain when he reached the café. Neither man noticed Bubba when he walked through the door; both men were too busy trying to throw the other off their game by trading verbal shots.

"They're lucky Sherry ain't here. She'd send both of them to their rooms without their supper," Bubba said, laughing to himself.

It was almost comical the way the two grown men went after each other. It was nearly like losing the game would mean the end of the world to the other. Bubba was just happy that Carpenter wasn't part of the night's entertainment. He would be there soon enough and then there would really be a free-for-all.

"Just what in the hell did I get myself into?" he thought to himself before ordering him and Jester a bite to eat.

"My goodness, are you going to move sometime this year, Boulet?" the pilot asked.

"Patience Moore," then Boulet said something no one understood.

"What damn language was that?" Moore wanted to know.

"It's Hebrew! Roughly translated, check mate," the crafty old Captain said as he made his final move.

It wasn't long before the two men joined Bubba and Jester at their table. He was just finishing his meal while they were ordering theirs.

"What did your man say?" was the first question Boulet had for his new deckhand.

"I had my sister wire him an airplane ticket. He'll be in Cancun day after tomorrow," Bubba reported.

"I have to pick up the mail and make a delivery. If you want to hitch a ride we can pick up your friend," Moore offered.

"Pick up the mail," Bubba said.

"Yes, believe it or not, two days a week I am the Mexican version of UPS," the pilot said, filling his new friend in. Bubba agreed and the deal was done.

"If you want McBride, there's a cantina down the street," Boulet informed the cowboy.

"Thanks anyway Captain, I gave it up awhile back," Bubba explained.

"Aren't we a pair to draw to: a cowboy that don't drink and an old hippy that don't get high. What do you think about that?" Boulet said with a laugh.

"I'm afraid Captain that the Jester and our new sailor are going to take up the slack," Bubba mentioned.

The part about the man's dog garnered a strange look from the two men. Bubba couldn't help but laugh. "Last time the two of them got together, it was not pretty. We're gonna have to keep them on a short leash," he told the men.

Later that night, Boulet told the cowboy that he and his dog could bunk on board The Third Coast. "What the hell, she's going to be yours anyway. You might as well get used to each other. We might even take her out in the morning," the old Captain added.

Three hours before the sun came up, Boulet was moving about on the top deck. After awhile, he moved below toward the sleeping quarters.

"All right you two; up and at 'em. I'm gonna teach you how to sail today." The old Captain no sooner got those words out of his mouth when he felt the sharp edge of a knife against his throat. "McBride, McBride. It's me, Boulet," he said quite loudly.

A hand reached out and turned on a light switch. Bubba was still holding his K-bar knife in his hand. "I am so sorry, Captain," Bubba said out of shock at his own actions.

"No, no McBride. Let that be a lesson to an old fool. How many tours did you do?" Boulet asked without answering the first question, "Were you in Nam?" He already knew the answer to that one.

"Two, one for my country and one for my men," answered Bubba. Then he asked, "Yourself?"

"I'm sorry to say I was on the other side of that war," Boulet confessed.

"Don't be sorry. Hell if I knew then what I know now, I might have been on that side," Bubba stated.

"That has not happened to me in a long time, Captain. I suppose it's being on the river, out in the jungle. I swear to God it looks just like Vietnam. If you want me to go sir, I wouldn't blame you," Bubba said half ashamed of his behavior.

Boulet rolled up his shirt sleeves to reveal his old track marks from his years of addiction. "McBride, we both have scars from that point in time, but we survived the wars both on the outside and inside of ourselves. Screw it, let's go fishing."

With those few word, Boulet went topside and fired The Third Coast's engine up.

A day later Bubba was back in the air, on his way to pick up his old war buddy in Cancun. His only hope was they could get there before Carpenter had a chance to fall in love again. He tended to do that on a regular basis. Hard drinking would ensue after the wheels fell off. Other than that, he was good as gold when he was on the straight and narrow.

Bubba was lucky they arrived thirty minutes before Carpenter's plane. It had been at least a year since they had seen each other.

"What did you volunteer me for, Sarge. I hope it wasn't the Priesthood," was the first question Carpenter asked.

"Nope worse than that: work," Bubba joked.

Carpenter took to The Deliverance right away and Captain Boulet took to him. Bubba had to learn sailing from the bottom up. He and Jester got the brunt of the grunt work and since Jester had no thumbs, it was Bubba on the other end of the mop.

Boulet had a lucrative contract with a number of grocery stores in the island chain. He would bring in fresh produce and other products from mainland Mexico. It wasn't as sexy as running guns to the rebels, like a few years earlier, but it was a damn sight safer.

While it was true Carpenter was the Captain's fair-haired boy on the water, it was Bubba who rocked at each port. The island folk had never seen an authentic cowboy in person. The only one they ever saw was on TV or the silver screen.

The word would pass through the villages like wild fire. In a matter of moments after their arrival, every man, woman and child would line the docks to catch sight of the cowboy. It was all new for Bubba; he was never known as the life of the party.

Boulet, after seeing this phenomena occur for the third time, suggested Bubba tell a story to the crowd.

"Captain, I don't know nothing about no story telling," he protested.

"Ain't much to it, just tell something that happened to you on the ranch," Carpenter said, chiming in.

Bubba finally gave in, "Alright if we get a crowd at our next stop, I'll give it a shot," he told the Captain, and his friend.

Sure enough, Bubba had no sooner got the boat tied off and the people began to gather. He jumped up on a crate and began to spin his yarn. The whole thing didn't last over ten minutes. The crowd began to hoot and holler when he had finished. Hearing the cheers, he was downright proud of himself.

"How was my story this afternoon, Captain?" Bubba asked smiling ear to ear.

"McBride, you need to work on your delivery. It was the most boring story I ever heard," said Boulet who wasn't known for pulling his punches.

"But Captain, you didn't hear them; they seemed to like it," Bubba argued.

"I hate to bust your bubble," said Boulet, cluing his deckhand in. "But ninety percent of those people no speaky no English."

Such a review might have discouraged anyone else from trying again, but Bubba was stubborn. He was up most of the night trying to hone his public speaking skills. The very next afternoon, not only did he tell the story of his life, he did so in Spanish.

"Hell of job, McBride. I have no idea what you told them but they understood and liked it," the Captain said giving Bubba his due.

Bubba was thrilled with his second performance, so much so that he began to work even harder on it. He tried telling the same story over and over at first. It didn't work too well because he found himself getting bored. Every day from then on, he entertained the island folks with different tales of a working cowboy and his dog. It would prove to be a skill that would serve him well in the years to come.

Seven weeks into Bubba Lee's indentured servitude, the old Captain decided it was time to change boats. His cowboy deckhand was doing so well that he thought it was time to move Bubba's classroom over to The Third Coast. It was time the man got the feel of his own boat under him. It was one part of the reasons the rest of Boulet's reasoning would come in time.

"You boys transfer what we need for some short deliveries over The Third Coast; it's time she starts pulling her weight," Boulet ordered the crew. I'm going to town to make a few business calls."

It was the truth, more or less. He did have to call a few of his customers, but the real reason was that he had been sent word that Bubba's adopted sister wanted a word with the good Captain. He knew from the way the cowboy talked about her that she wasn't one to be left waiting.

Sherry had but one simple request, and knowing the story as well as he did, he couldn't help but honor it. By the time Boulet had finished his conversation, he knew firsthand how Bubba got so good at taking orders. "Yes Ma'am and no Ma'am" was the extent of his part of the conversation.

The next morning The Third Coast set sail. It would be the last time Boulet would ever skipper her and in a way, that saddened him. They had weathered many a storm together in their twenty-some-odd years on the sea. But it helped knowing that she was going to a man that he had trained himself. He knew Bubba would take good care of her.

They sailed up the coast to Veracruz where they picked up a small load of produce to be delivered in San Juan. From a cannery in San Juan, they sailed to the Caribbean chain. The Third Coast then picked up a load of American freshly slaughtered beef for a special delivery.

About that time, the old Captain clammed up. Neither Bubba nor Jon knew where they were going. They did know the old Captain had some very colorful customers in the past; customers who thought a little gunplay was just a part of everyday life.

Bubba had carried a forty-five in his duffle bag ever since Nam. He prayed there would be no reason to see if the damn thing still worked. In his former life as a cowhand, it would be part of his job to protect the beef. "But at sea, you've got to be kidding," he thought to himself.

It was earlier in the evening when the Captain called for Bubba who was below deck. Jester was the first to appear through the hatch. The next thing the Captain saw was a cowboy hat, then a head and then, the complete man.

"McBride, I want you to guide her down the channel," Boulet exclaimed backing away from the wheel.

Bubba noticed something different about this particular harbor. He had been there before and not with the Captain. Jester happily began to bark. Bubba had no idea what had gotten into his friend, until he caught sight of the docks. He couldn't believe his eyes. There waiting for him to return from the sea was Sherry.

"She's all yours now," Boulet whispered into the cowboy's ear.

"Did you think I was going to let you and Jester miss my grand opening?" Sherry said as she hugged him when The Third Coast had been tied off in her new slip.

"You boys best be getting that beef unloaded if you want to eat tonight," Boulet ordered his crew.

"Damn you're a sly one, Captain," Bubba said laughing.

The whole island showed up that night for the opening of Sherry's Yellow Rose Café. Jim Moore had made it a point to be among the patrons.

"I never miss a free meal," he joked with Bubba as he handed him the bill.

All who came to Sherry's shindig that night found that Bubba wasn't lying about her cooking. Those who came would come again and again to feast on

Texas' fine food. The Coco Nut Telegraph was abuzz with the news for days (in Buffett talk).

The old Captain thought the night would end much better on a story. To Sherry's surprise, it was Bubba, not the Captain, who rose from his seat. Bubba relayed a story that one of his friends had lived. The story was about a yellow stallion that no man could ride. The evening saw the rise of two island legends: Sherry's café and the man who the island would come to know as Captain Cowboy.

"I still think it sounds like a damn comic book hero," Bubba said, confiding in the old Captain.

One by one, the crowd began to filter out toward the end of the evening. Carpenter and Jester were enjoying the bar aspect at one side of the Yellow Rose. Boulet was playing a game of chess with the one-time Alaska Bush pilot.

Bubba and Sherry decided it would a perfect time for a walk. The next thing they knew, they were at the docks. Bubba thought it would be the perfect time to show her his new boat. She loved everything about the craft except the name.

"What kind of name is The Third Coast?" she wanted to know.

"I don't know, I would guess it has a special meaning to Boulet," he answered.

"You mean you can rename her if you want?" was her next question.

"I suppose so," Bubba guessed.

"What would you name her Bubba, if you were to," was her last question.

Bubba thought for a moment before answering. "Considering the new Captain, the first mate who falls in love at a drop of a hat, and semi-sober canine, what about The Texas Ship of Fools," he said with a laugh.

"Are you joking?" she wanted to know.

"I don't know, you must admit it has a little ring of truth to it," he stated.

Bubba Lee and Jon would return and sail another four months with Captain Boulet. Bubba wouldn't leave until the Captain told him he was ready, and for that matter, the Captain wouldn't let the cowboy go until he was sure he was ready.

The two men, who had come from such different backgrounds and whose only thread of commonality was the times in which they lived, became like brothers. In a way, they were, as sons of a mother: Mother Ocean.

Sherry couldn't help but laugh when Bubba and his crew sailed into port on the newly renamed, The Texas Ship of Fools.

REASONING WITH A HURRICANE

Chapter 4

Years came and went like the tide. Bubba's charter fishing service went off without a hitch.

"It's hard to resist hiring a boat named the Texas Ship of Fools; it's like turning away from a train wreck," one of Bubba's customers was quoted as saying in a joking manner. It wasn't only the name of the boat, it was the huge mutt that could always be found sleeping in her galley. It also didn't hurt that his little sister was the finest cook in the entire island chain. Bubba Lee was living his dream.

The boat's success was only eclipsed by that of the Yellow Rose Café. It didn't matter if it was the tourist season or not, people still flocked to the place. Part of the reason for its popularity was that the one-time-cowboy-turned sea-Captain had evolved into a legendary story teller. Captain Cowboy had become the pied piper of the Caribbean and when he was in port, there was only standing room at the Yellow Rose.

Some would argue they came for the entertainment, but they would get rebuffed by Bubba. "It ain't me, I just hold down a bar stool. It's Sherry's cooking, I ought to know; I've been enjoying it most of my life," he would say, giving credit where credit was due.

He could also boast about being the only one, other than Sherry, with a key to the joint. The reasoning for the key would differ depending on who you asked. In the end, Sherry's answer was the closest to the truth.

"I just got sick and tired of being woke up after a late night card game or when the crew on the Texas Ship of Fools blew into port. If it's an unreasonable hour and they're hungry, they can damn well fix it themselves," she would say, setting the record straight.

Bubba had done a one-eighty since moving to the islands. Anyone who knew him as a child would confirm Bubba Lee was a man in a boy's body. The salt air of the ocean seemed to have the opposite effect; he was acting like a boy in a man's body. The one, who once was the stoic figure in the room, had become the star attraction.

No one was any happier than he was about having the childhood that had been stolen from him than Sherry was, but it was becoming a little bit of a pain in her backside. She always was the closest to him, but she was feeling more like his mother than his adopted sister. She told herself at first that it was just a phase; the onset of a premature mid-life crisis. Years had passed and the Bubba phase had taken root.

Bubba's maturity level wasn't the only thing that had changed; somewhere between a fishing trip and one his stories, Sherry's life got fuller. A young, dashing sea captain had swept her off her feet, when he wasn't looking. Bubba was feeling like the third man out.

She was always with him whenever he was in port and when he wasn't in port, she was always thinking about him. Bubba had long since forgotten what it was like to be in love. He had tried it once and it had left a bitter taste in his mouth.

He was set in his ways and change was not his strong suit. No one asked him what he thought or even for his blessing. The reality was Bubba hadn't had to share her with anyone in a long time. He didn't like it and he damn sure wasn't use to it.

It was part of it, but not all of it. Captain Tony Frenic was everything Bubba Lee wasn't. He was the real McCoy when it came to sea captains. Bubba was just a cowboy who read a book and decided he'd like to play captain in the big water. The whole damn affair was leaving him feeling insecure.

All the bad feelings he was having was coming out of the pleasure-seeking, me-first side of his brain. He had another side, a more rational side that was talking to him as well.

He would try his best to listen to that part of himself that had all the good sense: the part that told him she had a life, a private life that was none of his concern and the part that told him she had boyfriends in the past and they never bothered him before. More importantly, in the deepest reaches of his soul, he was actually happy for her.

It was driving him absolutely crazy having such competing voices in his head. A wide void was growing between his heart and his mind. He had always done the right thing in the past, especially when it came to Sherry. Why was it so difficult this time, why couldn't he let go? Those were just a few of the questions that preyed on him when he was alone with his thoughts.

Sometimes when two people are so close emotionally, they just take it for granted that the other party sees the situation the same way as they do. Bubba and Sherry both had forgotten they were incapable of seeing life from the same lens. He didn't see his child-like behavior and she didn't see his insecurities. Not seeing and making such assumptions was more or less like getting real close to a powder keg with a lit match. It was bound to blow up sooner or later.

The combustion point came out of an innocent gesture. Captain Frenic had set sail for the mainland early on a Sunday morning. Sherry was walking back from seeing him off when she passed the Texas Ship of Fools. She saw Jester laid out like a throw rug on the deck and took it as a sure sign Bubba was close by.

"Bubba, Bubba Lee. Come out from wherever you are," she called out like she had when they were children.

Directly his head popped out of the hatch. "Ma'am, it only looks like I'm hiding," he said, playing along with her.

It seemed like for awhile on the deck of his boat that things were as they had always been. Perhaps it was just too early for bad feelings to be awakened, or maybe it was true what they say about the Lord's day bringing out the best in everyone.

"I was thinking Bubba, it has been awhile since we had a good sit-down dinner; you know, just you and me, you too Jester," she said as she bent down to stroke his black, shiny coat.

"Sounds good to me Sis, you just tell us when and where," Bubba replied.

"Tonight, say about seven," she told him.

"You're the boss, we're just in it for the cooking," he said in a playful way.

Everything would have been grand if not for the twelve hours between the invite and the actual meal. Humans, given too much time to think, have the natural ability to screw shit up.

The remainder of Bubba's day was filled with the thoughts of how he was going to tell her how he had been feeling. Someone had once told him thoughts were neither bad nor good, it was what you did with them. He was sure if he could just tell her how he was feeling, they could work through it.

Sherry was doing pretty much the same thing as she prepared for that evening. It would be some kind of a task walking the line between telling Bubba it was alright to have a good time, but not to overdo it and be a pain in her ass. He always had a tendency to be over sensitive and take matters the wrong way.

The evening began innocently enough. Bubba and his loyal, four-legged companion were met at the door by Sherry wearing a dress he hadn't seen before. He was offered his favorite mason jar with ice tea, and not just any ice tea. It was Sherry's special ice tea, the very same that she used to wean Bubba off of the whisky. The night had all the makings of one kept in the memory banks, if only he could keep from messing it up.

He did alright at first, joking a little saying, "Yes Ma'am and thank you Ma'am," like every Texas boy of his age had been taught. They sat down to a steak dinner with all the fixings. She knew his favorite cut of beef was the Porter House steak and always kept a few on hand.

They both had something they wanted to get off their chest but neither knew how or where to start. Sherry thought a little small talk might be best to start out with. If she'd known that what she considered small talk was adding fuel to the fire, she might have chosen a different subject.

She began with talking about her love interest: where he had gone and the shipment that he was picking up. She spoke of the movie they had watched together and how he made her laugh.

"And by the way Bubba, did you notice my new dress? Tony bought it for me; he called it a present for our second-week anniversary," she told him.

It was beginning to feel like every third word out of her mouth was Tony. It was kind of the last name

Bubba needed to hear at the time, it was like rubbing salt in his wound.

"Who is this guy? The next thing she's going to tell me is the son-of-a-bitch walks on water," he thought to himself, forgetting how it felt to be in love.

He had never been pushed to his breaking point and that was saying something, after all he had been through. He might have bent a little a time or two but never broke. Every time she spoke the goody-two-shoes Captain's name, he got a little closer.

"Enough Sherry, can we change the subject," he said a little louder than he wanted to.

"Why Bubba Lee, is there something wrong?" she asked without a clue.

"Yes, yes there is. I came over here tonight because something has been eating at me. It has a lot to do with what is happening between us, I feel like you are slipping away from me. I thought we would be alone and we could talk this through," Bubba said, letting his guard down with the only person he ever felt safe enough to do it with.

"Have you lost your mind Bubba, we are alone," she said getting a bit hot herself.

"Hell, you and I ain't been alone since we sat down to eat. I know the Captain is gone but he might as well have passed me the beans the way you're going on about him. He's not even here and I still feel like the odd man out," he said, pointing out the picture as he saw it.

"I believe Bubba is just a little jealous. No wonder you've been acting like a ten-year-old," she fired back.

"Jealous? Now who's losing their mind? My God you are my sister, in every............" Bubba's voice trailed off, almost putting her feelings a head of his.

Bubba wasn't really mad but he was hurt. The more he said, the worse he knew he was going to feel about it. He could argue with her about the jealous part but the part about acting like a ten-year-old, he had to give her that.

Bubba might not have been mad but she had passed mad a few minutes earlier.

"Bubba, I am damned if I do and I am damned if I don't. I've spent hours today making your favorite dinner. If you didn't notice, it's the same one I made the first night you were home from war. I wore this dress for you 'cause I felt we hadn't spent enough time together. What more do you want?

"I'm not giving up or putting my life on hold until you can handle it and if you were thinking straight, you wouldn't ask me to." she said, blowing him away with both barrels.

"Sherry, I was hoping we might figure this out tonight. The words I had intended on saying were not the ones that came out. I believe I've raised the stakes far too high to resolve anything at this moment. Let me collect my dog and perhaps you can forgive me for my awkwardness. I wouldn't fight so hard if I didn't have everything to lose," he concluded and stepped out into the darkness of the night.

"Bubba you damn fool, you have nothing to lose," she said out loud but it was too late. He was already gone.

A memory came to her about the time she started doing the dishes. Some twenty years earlier, the roles played out that evening had been reversed. She was every bit of sixteen when Bubba told her he was going to get married.

She hit the replay button in her head and saw she had felt those same emotions. So in reality, they were not that different. All was forgiven before her memory tape reached its end.

"Damn you Bubba, I can't even stay mad at you," she said under her breath with a tender smile.

Sherry might have been able to forgive him but would Bubba be able to forgive himself. Nobody every kicked his ass as hard as he did when he was in the wrong. In his way of thinking, he couldn't have been more in the wrong. He was beginning to have his own interpretation on the phrase "paradise lost".

He sank into the sand replaying the argument that just transpired. How he wished he could turn back the clock but he knew in life there were no "do overs." He didn't know how he was going to move forward but he came to realize he couldn't do it there. He had been wrong thinking that she could fix it and make it better. It was going have to be an inside job. It was just impossible to live in the problem and fix it at the same time.

"Well Jester, what do you say we get out here for awhile," Bubba said rising to his feet and turning for home.

Bubba had a little house on a hill that overlooked the bay. He would stay there whenever he wasn't on a chartered fishing trip. Jon, his first mate, lived wherever he could find a warm bed. As of late that bed belonged to the woman who ran the bait shop.

It was nearing midnight when Bubba walked through his front door. Any other night he would have hit the rack and began anew with the morning. He was too upset for sleep and knew a few hours on the water would clear his head. He never realized what a tranquil effect the sea had until Captain Boulet pointed it out.

"It's the only drug no doctor can prescribe," the old Captain paraphrased from a Buffett song.

It didn't take long for him to grab a few things he might need. He was only going to be gone just long enough to get his head right and do a little soul searching. All he would need was a few clothes and perhaps a book or two. He kept the boat pretty well stocked so he wouldn't need to take much.

"I guess we better leave Sherry a note before we go," he told his dog.

Bubba didn't know much but he did know Sherry about as much as a man could know a woman. He knew she would set her clock a little earlier than usual. She would make it a point to walk up the hill to his house and tell him he was forgiven. He also knew he was probably forgiven before she went to bed but she would be mad if he bugged out without leaving a note.

He spelled out his reasoning pretty much in the note, telling her he was sorry and that he would get it together. He asked if they could talk about it when he returned. He then told her that deep down he was glad she had found someone like the good Captain. He ended with a simple, "I love you, Sis," and left the note on the table where he knew she would find it.

He threw his duffle bag over his shoulder, called to Jester, and walked out the door. He stopped for moment to gaze out over the town. Very few lights were on, but the ones that were sparkled like diamonds in his eyes. The crown jewel of the view was the flashing neon light at The Yellow Rose Café.

Someone had once asked her why she left the sign on all night when she was closed by 10 p.m.

"So Bubba and Jester can always find their way home," she answered without batting an eye.

He got a little teary eyed when he remembered what she had said; he always did. He took one last look before leaving for the boat.

"Come on Jester, we have miles to travel," he called to his dog as he was walking down the lane.

Bubba kept his eyes fixed toward the darkness as he guided his boat down the channel and out to sea. He passed a commercial fishing boat heading toward the docks. He thought it was strange to see the boat since he had spoken to her Captain a few days prior. He was under the impression the boat would be out to sea for a few weeks.

He didn't think much of it; if he had, he might have gone back and asked. A number of things could have caused the vessel to return to port. Someone on board could have needed medical attention or they might have returned for repairs that had gone overlooked. But Bubba was more concerned with his own boat and her heading.

"A sailor who worries about things other than his own duties aboard ship, is destined to sink or run aground," had been drilled into him by Boulet.

By 2:30 in the morning, The Texas Ship of Fools was well out to sea. The entirety of the past twenty-four hours was beginning to wear on Bubba. His eyes were growing heavy as the gentle sways of the boat rocked back and forth. He was starting to realize why the old sailors called the sea "Mother Ocean." It was because of her rocking motion.

He fought his urge to find his slumber as long as he could. He dropped anchor and turned his caution light on when he could fight no more.

"Alright Jester, you have the first watch. Try not to fall overboard," he mused.

The dog lifted his head up when he heard his master's voice. He saw Bubba's head dissappear below deck and followed him. The dog ran past Bubba and jumped on the bed as soon as the cabin's door was opened.

"I thought you were gonna stand watch. Whatever. I'm too exhausted to argue the point. I've done all the arguing I care to," he said as he looked at the picture of Sherry hanging over his bunk.

"Not a damn thing stupid about you is there boy. I'll see you in the morning," he said as he patted his faithful companion on the head.

The next morning before the sun was up Sherry was making her way to Bubba's house, just as he had predicted. She knew from a lifetime of experience that if she didn't tell him all was well, he would beat himself up about it.

"No one kicks your ass as hard as you do. You would surely kill the man that treated you that bad," she had long ago told him when she was trying to get him to sober up. The only thing that had changed was that he had put the plug in the jug.

The light was on in the front room. Like her, he had always been an early riser, something that seems to be in most Texan's DNA. The chances were extremely high Bubba Lee already had a pot of coffee brewed. She thought nothing of letting herself in.

She thought it odd the lights were on and there was no Bubba in sight. She thought at first he had a late night of replaying their little spat; he and Jester were probably fast asleep in the bedroom. She peeked in only to find his bed had not been slept in. She scanned the front room again, her eyes stopping when they reached the note on the table.

She read the note quietly to herself and then put it in her pocket. She was not surprised; he might have been behaving like an extrovert, but deep down Bubba Lee would always be a loner. He was always the type that needed to work things out between his own ears. It was not her first rodeo and not the first time he had gone off to sort life out.

Go with the angels," she said under her breath and went off to work.

She had been at The Yellow Rose for over an hour. The sun was up and the breakfast run had barely started. It was the off season so she was very busy. Sherry had been in the kitchen getting orders ready and not heard the scuttlebutt.

The swinging doors leading from the dining room to the kitchen swung open. A confused Jon Carpenter stood before her.

"Tell me that Bubba just moved the boat to the other side of the island," the man said, almost pleading with her.

"No, I don't think so. We kind of had us a little tiff last night. I found this note this morning saying he needed some alone time," she answered pulling the note from her pocket.

Hearing the news, the man's face turned pale as though all the blood had drained from it.

"Damn it, that back-assword cowboy. Sometimes I wonder who's gonna be the death of who. Didn't it dawn on him to check on the weather before he set sail?" Carpenter asked.

"Jon you're starting to scare me; now tell me what's wrong," Sherry demanded.

"On your way in this morning, didn't you notice the harbor was full, or that the storm flags were flying?" he asked. "Of course not, it was still dark when I left for work," she stated with a worried look.

"Evidently neither did your Bubba. A hurricane is brewing just east of here, a category one now but growing. I'm afraid if I am right, he's headed right into it," he said, letting his worries be known.

"How do you know where he's going?" Sherry questioned with tears in her eyes.

"Awhile back me and Bubba got our hands on a new depth finder," explained Carpenter. "We thought we'd go out for a few days and play with it. We came across this small island while we were out. It wasn't much, maybe a few thousand square feet.

"You know Bubba, he got all Texan about it and claimed her. New Texas is what he called the place. Sometimes when you are not looking, he can be downright goofy. Anyway, we went back on our off-time and built a small shelter. Bubba said it was going to be his little getaway.

"If everything happened last night like you said, I am certain that is where he's headed. I'd like to be wrong, but I ain't," he said, heading back out the swinging doors after he had expressed his fears to her. "Where are you going now? You can't just come in here and get me all worked up and worried, and then leave. Where are you going?" she asked.

"To the Coast Guard station. I'm going to see if I can get Bubba on the radio before it's too late," Carpenter old her.

"Wait a minute, I'm going with you," came her response.

It was already too late for the one-man, one-dog crew of the Texas Ship of Fools. Bubba had the rude awakening of being flung across the cabin. He opened his eyes and tried to focus, and looked for his dog. He found Jester was having problems of his own trying to gain his footing.

"Damn son. What the hell did we hit?" Bubba asked out loud.

The boat continued its violent side-to-side motion. Rain beat down like rocks on the craft. It was only the echoing sounds of thunder that drown out the sound of the relentless rain.

"Seems we've run into a bit of a squall," Bubba explained. "Hell, it sounds like real turd-floater, don't it now?"

He pulled his way over to where he kept his rain gear. He knew he had to get topside for a status report. He also knew if the waves were as high as they felt, he'd have to right the ship. Boulet had taught the cowboy to drive his boat directly into the surf.

"McBride you let one of those twenty-foot waves hit you broad side and you're liable to capsize," the old Captain's words were ringing in his ears.

Bubba finally got his rain gear on after a bit of a struggle. He had no idea what he would find above deck so he told his dog to stay down below. All he needed was a monster wave to take his best friend over the side.

It wasn't as simple as a little storm that blew up during the wee hours of the morning. What he found topside was a full-fledged hurricane. He had heard the old sailors in the village refer to storms such as the one Bubba found waiting on him and their stories were not the tales you put children to bed with.

At first all Bubba could do was stand there in amazement of it all, then something inside him snapped. "You dumb ass, this ain't the time to be gawking," he said to himself and snapped into action. He then fought his way to the bridge and brought her helm about.

Trying his best to stay a move ahead of the storm, he reached into his rigging box and pulled forth a piece of rope. In half-hitch knots he tied himself in place and waited for the battle.

The wind blew off the ocean in a gale force, as freezing rain drops stung his unprotect face. The waves as big as mountains washed over the bow, one right after another. A few hours passed as though they had no end. He looked at his watch; the hand read ten in the morning but the darkness made it seem like ten at night.

Far away from his thoughts were the reasons that had brought him to sea in the first place. He knew if he and Jester stood any chance, he would have to keep his mind clear and on the problem at hand. Sherry would always be there, it was up to him to make sure he was.

Jon Carpenter and Sherry came bursting into the Coast Guard station. The sailors of station 79502 sat around a table drinking coffee.

"Where is Captain Cowboy? It's boring as hell around her;, we could use one of his stories," one of the men popped off.

"I got something for you that will damn sure break your boredom," said Carpenter, losing his cool. "Bubba Lee's out there, somewhere. So why don't you boys stop treating today like you're on vacation and find the boy?"

"What! Did he lose his ever-loving mind? It ain't a category 1 anymore; she's done hit warm water.

117

She's a category 3 working on 4. What in the hell was he thinking," a man stated while jumping to attention.

"No, Bubba isn't crazy. Yes it was foolish, but he didn't know about your freaking storm," Sherry said, crying while she was behind Carpenter.

"Sorry Sherry, we didn't see you. Come on boys let's see if we can't find her crazy-ass cowboy for her," the Coast Guard Captain said seeing the woman's tears.

"I have a general idea where he was headed," said Jon Carpenter, who was a little more calm this time when he spoke. "Now if I could just see your chart."

Carpenter told Sherry it was best if she went back to the Yellow Rose. She would be better off staying busy. She'd only get depressed if she stayed at the station watching the clock. He promised to come get her when he heard something. She resisted a little before realizing he was right.

The Coast Guard Captain waited until she was gone before rolling out the chart. Carpenter studied the chart knowing it meant life or death. "Right here, there's a small island here and I think it's where he was headed," he pointed out.

"Jon, I sure hope you're wrong. Look at this, he's headed right for her," said the Captain while showing the man the radar.

They both agreed their next step was to try to raise Bubba on the radio. "Coast Guard station 79502. Ship of Fools. Do you copy?" the radio man repeated over and over to no answer.

Bubba was up to his neck in trouble and nowhere near the two-way radio. Noon had come and gone with no letup in the storm. His body was numb from his head down. He didn't know if he was winning or losing the battle but at least he and Jester were still a float.

It was some time in the fifth hour when the storm broke. Bubba looked up and suddenly the sky was clear. It was as though the whole day was a bad dream, if he wasn't soaking wet he might have believed it.

He took a deep breath and went below to check on his dog and get a bite to eat. He had a sandwich, fed Jester and laid down on his bunk. "Well boy, we did it. We came out of it in one piece," he told his four - legged friend.

It was about then when he heard his call signs and name on the boat's radio. "This is Coast Guard station, 79502. You copy? Texas Ship of Fools, come in Captain McBride. Damn it Bubba if you're out there, pick up the damn mic," came Jon Carpenter's voice.

"Would you keep it down, I've had a hard day," Bubba joked with his old friend.

"Bubba where the hell are you?" his relieved friend asked.

"Hell, I don't rightly know. I've been a bit busy fighting with this storm. I ain't had time to get my bearings. You can bet your ass I'm as lost as an Easter egg though. The good news is, man and dog are still kicking," he said, joking about his condition.

He had no sooner got those words out of his mouth when he heard all hell break loose again. Bubba wasn't out of the woods; he was merely in the eye of the storm. He had heard the old sailors call it, "Being in the belly of the bitch."

"Well boys I take it back; there's no good news, not today. She's back, and she's pissed. Got to go back topside, wish me luck. Jon, you know, tell Sherry," was Bubba's last transmission.

"You come home and tell her yourself," Carpenter said into the radio's microphone. It was too late; Bubba never heard his friend. The boat's radio had shorted out in the storm.

"Alright Jester you know the drill, you stay below deck," he told the dog before he went topside.

The back side of the hurricane was just as ugly as her front side. Monster waves swallowed the deck at will, lightning filled the sky with a strobe-light effect and thunder made it sound like the Gods were at war. The only event in Bubba's life that came close was one particular firefight in Vietnam.

Back on the island, people were starting to gather at the Yellow Rose. They had heard their Captain Cowboy was missing and wanted Sherry to know their prayers were with her. A vigil of sorts was being held for the cowboy and his dog.

Carpenter had been up to tell her he had spoken to Bubba and that he was alright at the time they had spoken. He told her Bubba was halfway through the storm and the boat was holding its own. He said as soon as the warnings were lifted, the Coast Guard would begin the search. The man returned to the Coast Guard station as soon as he delivered his message of hope.

Bubba felt a lot better after speaking with Carpenter. He had been worried about the hell Sherry must have been going through. If he'd only waited until morning but it was just a little late for second thoughts.

He was grateful his old friend was there to look after her. Years earlier, in the jungles of Southeast Asia, they had made a pact. Carpenter would see after Sherry if something ever happened to him. The thought alone offered Bubba a measure of comfort as he battled the storm.

Night time engulfed the Texas Ship of Fools and the storm had no end in sight. The wind still was at gale force and the rain seemed unmerciful. Bubba Lee didn't know how much more he or his boat could handle. He knew it was out of his hands; about all he could do was pray and hope for the best.

Suddenly lightning struck the main mast. The pole that held the sail in place had broke in two. The top of the huge pole came crashing down and went right through the deck.

"Lord, this is not the answer I was hoping for," Bubba yelled at the heavens.

He tied the ship's wheel off best he could so he could go below and inspect the damage. Bubba wasn't at all looking forward to what he found. The mast pole had not only pierced the upper deck but had gone completely through the hull. Water was rushing in from all around the boat's wound.

Boulet had conveyed to him the story about running from the authorities and having to deal with a bullet hole in her hull. The two differing factors between the incidents were that Boulet had a fairly good idea where he was and it was only a bullet hole. Bubba Lee had no clue where he was and there was a twelve-inch-in-diameter pole sticking through her hull.

He grabbed everything he could think of to stuff into the hole in the hull. The human body and a hull of a boat are just the opposite when wounded. In the human body, it is essential to keep fluids (blood) from running out. Bubba was trying his best to keep them from running in. He turned his pumps on when he had finished with her hull.

He had been so preoccupied with the boat's damage that he hadn't noticed the raging storm had died down. When he did, he saw that one thing in his favor. However, even though he did the best he could with the Texas Ship of Fools, he knew he had only managed to put her on life-support. Her wounds were fatal.

The boat was sinking, the only thing he could do was prolong it long enough to do what he needed to do. The boat had an eighteen-foot dingy on deck that he lowered into the water. A year earlier he had been in an arms surplus store in Tampa where he had purchased three inflatable life rafts.

His first task was not to run to the radio and start crying "May Day!" The boat was going down and unless he wanted to go down with it, he would have to be prepared. Staying focused and managing his time was his first and last order of business.

He inflated all his army surplus rafts and checked them all for leaks. He didn't see the need for jumping off one sinking ship onto another sinking raft. Then he tied all his rafts together, giving a whole new meaning to the word, "flotilla".

The next stop he had was in the galley where he began to prioritize the essential food needs. He put the perishables in the ice chest and placed them in the raft closest to the dingy. He and Jester would have to eat those first and whatever spoiled would become fish bait. All the other non-perishables would go in boxes and in the rafts.

The next essential going into Bubba's floating island was fresh water. He always kept five thirty-gallon drums on board. His task was to get those above deck and distributed into his rafts, where the weight would not be a problem.

Shelter came after food and water. He retrieved the smallest of the canvas sails, rolled it up with some aluminum rods and flung them into the dingy. Blankets, a first-aid kit, fishing poles, his pistol, rifle and other such items would be stowed away in the dingy.

It was a free for all after the essentials for life were all transferred. A six-inch battery-powered TV, an AM/FM radio, a Coleman stove and whatever else he could think of. The books he loved went as well. He had no idea how long he'd be adrift, so he thought reading would help occupy his mind. The last to go was the picture of his Sherry that hung over his bunk.

It was only after he had accomplished what he set out to do that he went to the radio. "May Day, May Day," he said over and over. "This is The Texas Ship of Fools signing off . May God go with me and all I love," he announced into the radio's microphone for the last time.

He gently placed his beloved dog in the dingy and was fixing to join him when an idea hit him. "Hold on boy, I'll be right back," he told his pooch. Bubba rushed down below and got a five gallon can full of diesel and began to poor it on his sinking boat. He then jumped in the dingy and rowed out. He found his flair gun and when he was at a safe distance away, he fired it into the boat, setting the whole thing ablaze.

"Sorry old girl! Jester, I just hope someone might see the fire and come find us," he said, explaining his reason for setting the boat on fire.

In silence, the cowboy watched his dream literally go up in smoke. He thought about Captain Boulet and how disappointed he would be. Watching The Texas Ship of fools go down in flames was like watching the death of a loved one. Bubba Lee could not help but feel guilty.

She didn't burn long before the ocean claimed her. No one came and the exhaustion of it all drove Bubba into a deep sleep. He and his dog were lost, but were they lost to the world?

NOT FORGOTTEN

Chapter 5

Dawn found Sherry on the pier the morning after Bubba and Jester had been lost in the hurricane. She was gazing out over the water with a hot cup of coffee in her hand. Sleep hadn't been hers the night before because of her worries. She refused to allow herself to think the worse but she worried nonetheless.

"Bubba, I would give anything to know where you are. Be safe and come home to me," she whispered on the wind. She thought she was alone but she was startled by a sound behind her.

"I don't mean to intrude, I thought I would come tell you that the Coast Guard is headed out for the search," Jon Carpenter explained.

"How did you know where to find me?" she asked in a melancholy tone.

"I figured you would be down here. To tell you the truth, I've been down here two or three times during the night, expecting every time to see that crazy cowboy coming up the channel with his old dog barking the whole way," the man confessed.

"Jon, do you believe in God?" Sherry asked as she turned to face him with tears in her eyes.

"I guess I must. I have been talking with him all night. I reckon we're pretty close to being on a first-name basis. You shouldn't worry so much, Sherry. God watches out for folks like Bubba; he didn't make too many of them," he said, explaining what he believed.

"I just hope the Good Lord likes a good story as much as we do," Sherry said between her tears.

Carpenter put his arms around her and wished at the moment that he could trade places with his old friend. "You get it all out, then we'll go see the boys at the Coast Guard station off," he said trying his best to comfort her.

Hours passed like days at the Yellow Rose. Every time the phone rang, Sherry would nearly come out of her skin. Other than the phone, the island was like a graveyard. Every now and then someone would pop in and see if there was any news.

It was almost like magic. Every time she felt like she was at her wit's end, the door would open and there would be a friend. They all told her not to worry, Bubba Lee would turn up.

Carpenter spent most of his time at the Coast Guard station, waiting for a bit of news - any news. Every hour on the hour, he would report to Sherry. He was worried about his friend but was also really getting worried about Sherry. Finally he got hold of Captain Tony as he was known on the island. He explained the happenings of the last day. He told Sherry's boyfriend it might be a good idea if he got back as soon as possible.

Carpenter knew that she would have his hide if she caught wind he was reaching out to Tony Frenic, but he was willing to take the heat. The man agreed with Carpenter and said he would be there as soon as he could.

It had already been a long day for everyone on the island, but more so for Sherry and Carpenter. It was the second such day in a row. Neither one of them knew how many days lay in store and how many more they could handle.

The sun had nearly set when Carpenter made the half-mile trek up to the Yellow Rose. He was hungry, tired and in need of a stiff drink. The last two on the list would have to wait until he had the remainder of the day squared away. The first thing he needed was food, but it was his secondary reason for the evening walk. The lady who owned the place, his best friend's adopted sister, was his primary concern.

Sherry was standing in the doorway waiting for him, just like she had been the twelve other times he had been there. The last trip went about the same as the other dozen had. She asked him if there had been any word and he'd have to tell her "no." Each time it felt like he died a little more inside.

The business at the Yellow Rose was beginning to pick up. Some people had dropped by to see if there had been any word from the search party. Others, like those who worked the docks and the local shipyard, were just getting off work. The Yellow Rose was the most popular place in town even on a slow night; mainly because the Yellow Rose also had a bar.

Carpenter sat at the booth where he and Bubba used to sit. It was strange to be there without him and old Jester, who went everywhere with Bubba. Just thinking about it made him sad but at least Bubba and Jester were together wherever they were.

Sherry brought him his supper. It was the first meal he had eaten in two days. She then sat across the booth from him. Carpenter was dead tired but he wasn't alone, from where he sat, he could tell she was too.

"Sherry, girl you need to go home and get some sleep. You cannot go on like this: worrying yourself sick. You ain't doing Bubba a bit of good running yourself into the ground. And to be very blunt, it's a hell of a job having to worry about both of you," he pointed out as he ate his chicken-fried steak.

Any other time and said by any other person, she would have been mad as hell. He was right though and she was just too tired to get mad. She put up a bit of a fight, but it was mostly for show.

Finally she relented, "I suppose you're right. A good, hot bath and a few hours of sleep sounds good about now. But if you hear anything, anything at all, you come wake me," she told him.

"I can't wait to tell Bubba. He ain't going to believe this, not in a million years," he said smiling.

"Tell Bubba what?" she asked with a confused look. "That you said I was right. He ain't going to believe it," he joked.

"Ha, ha" she said before grabbing her purse and leaving for home.

Bubba Lee woke up late in the morning on the second day. He rubbed he eyes and looked out to sea. He hoped the day before had only been a bad dream. The miles of nothingness told him the dream had only begun and it wasn't a good one at that.

The sight of his small dingy and her floating appendages brought the memories of the day before back. A week earlier, he was living the dream, as they say. He was the Captain of his own boat, a business man and a legendary story teller. It was all gone. He remembered seeing it sink the night before.

He was right back where he started from: just a man and his dog. He still had a dream, even though it had changed. He had awakened with a new dream, much simpler but harder to accomplish. His new dream was to get back and see Sherry. It would be the dream that would see him through the trials and tribulations that would surely follow.

The night before, he refused to go down with the ship; that morning he refused to allow his bad luck to bring him down emotionally. He had far too much to live for to throw in the towel. Bubba knew all he could do at the present time was to put a happy face on it and pray he was found.

Jester went to his master when he saw he was awake. "And a good morning to you," Bubba said after a good face licking. "Are you hungry boy? Hell, I am starving," he went on.

It dawned on him that other than a sandwich, the last real meal they had was at Sherry's some two days earlier. "What I'd give to have that night back," he said out loud. "I bet you would have a few things you would like to say to me, if only you could talk," he said to Jester. "Like 'This is another fine mess you got us in, Bubba,' " he said, giving his friend a voice.

"Enough crying over spilled milk. What do you say we have a good breakfast?" he said pulling one of the rafts up to the side of the dingy.

The first thing he pulled from the small raft was the camp stove. "What do you say boy, a little bacon and eggs. Nothing but the best for my crew," he joked.

Bubba was one castaway who was going to take full advantage of the twenty-first century as long as he could. He proved it by producing a small AM/FM radio from the raft and placing it in the bow of the dingy. The only station he could find was out of Havana, Cuba.

"What do you say Jester, a little Cuban salsa with your eggs," he said, once again making light of their situation.

The whole time Bubba busied himself, he kept an eye out for a passing ship or aircraft. It must have been a pretty bad hurricane; they had named it George. Bubba had a few other names he would've liked to call it. According to the Cuban announcer, Bubba and Jester were just two of the missing.

"One dumb-ass cowboy and his dog are probably not real high on their priority list," he thought but he kept an eye out nevertheless.

Breakfast was done and he sat down to eat. "Eat up son, it ain't as good as Sherry's but it's going to have to do," Bubba told his pooch.

They ate a hearty breakfast and then got down to the chores of the morning. Bubba washed and dried the dishes and Jester did whatever dogs do.

"Well what would you like to do next boy, the sky's the limit on this pleasure cruise. We can do a little fishing, go swimming, or even watch a little TV; that would be without the HBO I'm assuming," Bubba said remembering the small television.

His little jokes and the way he spoke to his dog was just the way he went about keeping his spirits up. It wasn't a scrape he had ever found himself in and more than likely it wouldn't be the last. He had a chance and that was more than the 112 people who died in the hurricane had.

"And the good news is Jester, just think of the story we are gonna have when we get home. They're going to be lined up outside the Yellow Rose just to see Captain Cowboy and his four-legged first mate ride again," Bubba exclaimed in a bold fashion before jumping into the ocean. "Come on in boy, the water feels good," he yelled out.

It was late in the afternoon and the sun was beginning to beat down on the water. Bubba had earlier fashioned together a makeshift shelter from the canvas sail he had brought with them. His morning project was working well, protecting the day-old castaways from the heat of the day.

Bubba had caught some nice-sized fish after his morning dip. He was in the process of cleaning them and watching a TV program out of Santa Domingo. All the Spanish he had learned on the ranch was serving him well. By then the news was proclaiming George the storm of the century. The death toll had risen to two-hundred by that evening.

His mind turned to Sherry once again, she must be worried sick. He was grateful he had left Carpenter behind; at least she wasn't alone. It was about that time that he had a brain storm.

He pulled one of the rafts close and began to rummage through its contents until he found a pen

135

and paper. He then repeated the exercise with the next raft until he found a bottle.

He thought for a moment before he put pen to paper. Bubba decided on two short messages; one for whomever might find the bottle and one for Sherry. In the first note, he explained his current situation and asked whoever found it to see to it that his beloved Sherry receive the second. He then added the date and the address to the Yellow Rose cafe at the bottom of the page.

In the second letter, he put more of his heart into it. He told her that he and Jester were fine and they couldn't wait to see her. He wrote that he was sorry for the words spoke in anger what seemed to be a lifetime ago. He ended with how much he loved her. He rolled both letters up and put them in the bottle. "Look Jester, the old message in a bottle trick," he said as he threw it as hard as he could. Bubba didn't know if it would work or not but he felt better.

The castaways feasted that night on Bubba's catch of the day. It wasn't long before the sun set on Bubba's first day adrift. The Captain and crew of the ill-fated Texas Ship of Fools would watch a little more television before calling it a day. Bubba prayed the days that followed would end just as well.

Sherry had been awakened at four in the morning by a call from an old friend that everyone in her world knew as Doc. Years earlier he had been her history professor in college although he wasn't much older than she was. They had stayed in touch over the years and she was happy when his first book about rodeo came out.

Doc's books about the men Bubba Lee used to run with naturally made McBride a fan. He and Sherry had driven all the way to Amarillo to a book signing a few years before they left Texas. Doc and Bubba hit it off right away, "Like two peas in a pod," was how she summed it up.

A year later, Bubba talked Doc into joining a secret society that he and his rodeo friends belonged to in Montana. The society was dedicated to the preservation of a sacred valley and a string of mustangs who had roamed there free for centuries.

"Hell Doc, if you're going to write about us, you might as well become one of us," was Bubba's recruitment speech.

Once a year Bubba Lee would fly to the mainland, meet Doc in Texas and then drive up to the Great Northwest for the gathering. Bubba said it was his one chance a year to be a cowboy again. Doc would usually come back to the island with Bubba when the gathering was over.

The ex-professor, a one-time cowboy and the best cook in the island chain had become somewhat of a family. It was the reason Sherry was pleased to get the call, even at four in the morning.

"Sherry, I know it's early but I tried all day yesterday to get Bubba on the phone. Then I heard on the news about George and I became a little concerned," the man said, explaining the early nature of his call.

"It's alright, I'm glad you called. I was going to call you anyway this morning. I don't know how to put this, but we lost Bubba Lee in the storm," she said halfway in tears.

"You mean Bubba's dead," the shocked man asked. "No, no, no I mean we lost him. He left in the night on the boat and we haven't been able to find him," she said trying to correct her prior statement.

She then told him everything that had led up to Bubba leaving three nights earlier and how he didn't know about the hurricane brewing out in the Atlantic. She told him Jon Carpenter had briefly spoken to him before the radio went dead. She ending by telling her old friend that the Coast Guard had gone out the day before, but she hadn't heard anything as of the moment. Through her tears, she told him everything. A short pause followed the conclusion of her story.

"Sherry, get someone to pick me up in Miami tomorrow. Perhaps Jim Moore if he's not busy. There's no sense in your going through this alone.

"I am certain that Bubba and that old mutt are fine. It's not the first time he's come up missing. Do you remember last year when he was MIA and come to find out, he and Jester were at a football game in New Orleans. Bubba only wished he was in a hurricane after you were through with him," Doc mused remembering one of the many times Bubba had found himself on her bad side.

Sherry laughed at the New Orleans story and afterwards she felt guilty for doing so. The man on the other end of the line somehow sensed it.

"Bubba loved to make you laugh, sometimes he relished making you mad, but never did he ever want you to cry. Now I have to go pack for my island vacation, and you need to get on the horn and get me a ride from Miami. We both know I can't swim," he said trying to cheer her up.

She thought about the conversation she had with Doc as she readied herself for work. He was right about cheering up. Bubba wasn't dead, not that she knew of anyway. So why was she behaving like he was?

"We could have kept a grave digger employed for life, all the times we thought the worse had happened to him," she told herself while looking in the mirror. "The minute I see his body is when I'll lose it. That's the way Bubba would tell me to handle it if he was here."

She found an older-looking Jon Carpenter waiting for her to open the Yellow Rose. The minute he saw her, he knew she wasn't the same woman he had sent home the night before.

"Have you heard any news this morning, Jon?" she asked as she turned the key in the door knob.

"No, not a peep all night," Carpenter answered. "It's like Bubba went down a rabbit hole and they went in after him,"

"Can you find me Jim Moore's phone number and bring it to me. I talked to Doc this morning and he's on his way down here. He needs someone to pick him up in Miami," she said, filling him in on the earlier phone call.

"Sherry, I can call Jim for you," Carpenter offered.

"No that's alright, I'll do it," said Sherry. "You get in here and let me fix you some breakfast. Then you can get me his number. After that, I want you to follow your own advice and get some sleep; I mean it. It pains me to say it, but you look like warmed-over dodo. And one more thing, thank you." With that she hugged his neck.

The day went about like the day before. The only difference was Sherry's frame of mind. It started to rub off on everyone else half way through the day. A man who came in for lunch asked her when they found Bubba. She pointed out unless he knew something she didn't, they hadn't. He said the only reason he asked was because of her uplifting mood.

"Sir, there were a lot of people killed in the storm, and my heart goes out to their families. I hear there's twice as many missing. It would be downright shameful of me to think my Bubba was the only one they presume is alive and, therefore, the only one they're looking for. I will get the news about him when I get it. Good or bad, I'll deal with it then," she explained.

Everyone at the café stood up and clapped after her little speech. The place seemed to come back to life from that moment on. If she, the one who loved him more than anyone, could have a stiff upper lip, then everyone could.

The ill-fated crew of the Texas Ship of Fools had been adrift for six days, without even a hint of a

141

rescue boat or a plane. Both sky and sea were absent of any human life. It was like the world had one void and Bubba Lee and Jester had found it. Each day the sun and the emptiness robbed him of a little more hope.

Bubba had kept a close eye on his supply of fresh water; it was the one necessity they couldn't live without. The sea would provide if their food supplies ran out. They had dinner as long as Bubba had his fishing pole.

Bubba thought the real torture would be if he had no water and yet was surrounded by water. It was true what the old sailors had said, "The ocean is the wettest desert on earth. A man can just as easily die of thirst in the middle of the Atlantic as he can in the Sahara Desert." By Bubba's crude calculations, they could go another week to ten days.

Bubba was beginning to worry about what came after the water was gone. He did his best to divorce himself from such depressing thoughts, but they kept seeping through: the God-awful questions a man can ask himself when time is the one item he has in abundance.

It was hard to keep a positive thought process with so little room in the dingy. A man in a prison cell had more room than the man who had grown up on the endless, high plains of Texas. It didn't help that all his gadgets of the twentieth century had ran out of battery power.

He was left too long with his somewhat crazy conversations with Jester. "What would you think if they dropped the bomb? You think we would know about it?" he'd asked.

"I guess if you asked, 'What was that?' you'd probably be alright," Bubba would answer for his speechless dog.

He'd spend the next hour trying to decipher his friend's thoughts by the way Jester looked at him. "And they call us dumb animals. This dumb-ass cowboy, who got both our butts in a pickle, wants to talk about the bomb. Come on Bubba, get it together," he said, surmising what the dog's thoughts were.

He was thinking about Sherry when he wasn't worrying Jester with some off-the-wall conversation. He began reliving their lives and looking for clues to the truth: the truth that would only come years later. It was a bit of truth he fought with over telling her or not telling her. The night of their argument he had almost let it slip. Perhaps he should have told her but that was not the time.

His thinking about the sister he left behind was just as nutty as his talks with the dog. He was wondering if he was cracking up or using the absurd as a diversion from the real depressing thoughts about what would happen in the end: how would they go out? Would he have what it took to end his friend's misery or his own for that matter. Day by day the absurd gave way to the uncertainty of life without rescue.

On the eighth night, the man who had walked through many valleys of evil was nearing his rope's end. Bubba knew by then the authorities had more than likely given up the search. He was a dead man who was still breathing. His death row had no walls or bars, just miles and miles of open water.

He felt helpless for the first time in his life. All the crazy things he could say to his dog and all his memories wouldn't make that feeling go away. The man's thoughts turned to the one who would mourn the news the most. He had done the unthinkable; he had broken Sherry's heart.

In silence he watched the sun fall from the sky for the eighth time from his little dingy. The darkness of the night seemed to be filled with the lost prayers of the ghost of those who had met the same fate.

Jester, being the ever loyal companion, put his head in his master's lap to comfort him. Bubba stroked his old friend's fur as he talked to him.

"Why the hell we ever left Texas is beyond me. I always figured I'd meet my end either by a rattlesnake bite or by a salty horse, not wasting away in the middle of nowhere.

I'm sorry boy, sorry for dragging you into this. I'm sorry I let you down. I wish I knew what tomorrow will bring. I pray a little hope," the saddened cowboy spoke.

Jester licked Bubba's hand as though he had understood every word and who's to say he didn't. Once again the man stared into the darkness, hoping above more than anything else, for resolution. One way or another, the story had to end before he went insane.

"A worry will wear your ass out quicker than a hard day's work and you won't have a damn thing to show for it." A voice from Bubba's past reached out and jerked him. It belonged to his first foreman, who had taught him cowboying from the ground up.

The man's name was Gordon Maatsch and he might have been the toughest human being the good Lord ever put in the saddle. Maatsch didn't stand for any whining. "Are you on or off the tit?" he would ask if Bubba complained about his work.

Bubba was about sixteen and working on the ranch after school. A cold front dropped the mercury to the bottom of the thermometer. Bubba was going on about how cold it was.

"Damn son, this ain't nothing, I grew up pulling calves in the coldest of Nebraska winters. You want to bitch, just think about the poor bastard who got my old job," the old foreman scolded.

Later in the bunk house, Maatsch saw the opportunity for a teachable moment. "Son, I don't care how bad you might think you have it. Somewhere out there is a man who has it a little worse than you. When you find yourself singing, 'Woe is me,' give some thought to him," the foreman said before the lights went out.

He hadn't thought of the old man in years, in fact he'd been dead for twenty. The last time he heard the man call out from the grave was when he was in a foxhole, once again praying not to die. Maatsch's words would have the same effect that night on the water. Bubba Lee knew that somewhere in the world there was someone who had it a bit worse than he did.

He rolled his bed out and thanked the old man for his timeless words. The last thought he had before drifting off to sleep was, "If the Lord came in the night for him, he'd be riding the River Jordan with Gordon Maatsch by morning." It wasn't such a bad thought for him to be having.

Day five of the disappearance of the small island's only celebrity came and went like the four that preceded it. Sherry and Jon Carpenter were still holding it together. Doc, her friend and writer, had flown in from the mainland a few days earlier. The Coast Guard hadn't reported news of any kind, good or bad. The folks around the Yellow Rose Café were holding to the old saying, "No news was good news."

The supper run had come and went but people were still milling around the bar. Sherry knew customers were hungry for something besides food or drink. It dawned on her they had gone days without a story. Bubba Lee had the island folk spoiled; they were "Jonesen" for a yarn.

It hit her like a bolt of lightning; Bubba was not there, but not ten feet away from her stood Doc, a noted novelist. She called her friend over to her. She asked him if he'd do the honors of standing in for the famed, but lost, Captain Cowboy.

"Sherry I don't tell stories, I write them," the man protested at first.

"Your telling me that all those years standing in front of a class, you never told one story," she fired back.

"No, I'm telling you that I have not spoken in public in some time, I might be rusty," he answered back. He then added, "What the hell, I'll give it a shot."

Sherry raised her hands and the Yellow Rose fell silent. "I know Bubba is not here with us tonight, but I am sure wherever he is, he's telling a story. I've asked Doc if he'd regale us with one his tales this evening. So with further ado, I give you Doc, the rodeo cowboy's scribe," she said in her introduction of Doc.

"With an intro like that, I don't know why Sherry's not before you all tonight, instead of me," he joked.

"Like your Captain Cowboy, I grew up in Texas, and, therefore, I grew up around cowboys. I idolize these 'knights of the plains.' I told myself if I ever was in the position, I'd buy me a little spread. I even had a name for it: The Hanging Tree Ranch. A few years ago, my dream came true, and my ranch is now a reality.

"That brings me to my story. The other morning about 5 a.m., I was getting ready to come here. The sun wasn't up and I had just started on my first cup of coffee. I just happened to look out my window and saw that one of my cows was out and standing on the road.

"Now friends, that was the last thing I needed that morning. So I went down to the barn and saddled my trusty horse Muffin Man. I'd be the first to tell you all that I ain't known for my skills with a rope. Usually when I get around a horse with a rope, one of us goes to the doctor, sometimes both.

"Here I go anyway, tearing out of the barn with rope in hand. It took about an hour to get my loop around that old hussy's neck. Well I dallyed up good around the saddle horn and began to drag her worthless hide home. By the time I got to the barn, the sun is up. I looked behind me and much to my surprise, it's not my cow. No friends, not my cow at all. It was the neighbor's wife and she was mad as an old wet hen, as we say back home," Doc finished to the roar of the crowd.

Sherry wore a smile all the way home after work. She had asked her friend to tell a story for her patrons and found she had gotten just as much out of it. Doc was no Bubba Lee, but then again, Bubba was no Doc. She began to miss her Bubba a little more that evening after the Yellow Rose had been graced with story time once again.

It was late in the evening when she walked through her door. She thought she'd take a hot bath and have a glass of wine before calling it a day. She spent a good hour relaxing in the tub, sipping a glass of white wine.

She was about to pour herself one last glass when she saw something under the couch. She had been the only one in the house since Bubba and Jester had been her guest, which seemed to her to be a lifetime earlier. "I wonder why I haven't noticed it," she said as she bent down to retrieve the flat object.

It was a book she found hiding under the sofa, and not just any book. It was the same book she had given Bubba Lee for his birthday back in Texas, the same book that had started the whole island madness, Jimmy Buffett's "Tales from Margaritaville".

"I wonder how you got under there," she asked out loud. It then dawned on her that she had borrowed the book months earlier from him and never found the time to read it. She remembered the look on Bubba's face when she asked to borrow it. He had the thing for years and she had only glanced through it.

"Why now, Sherry" he had asked curiously.

"I'd just like to see the blueprint why we are here," she halfway joked.

"It's a little late in the game for that don't you think? You're not having second thoughts are you?" he asked, still confused at the female mind.

"No Bubba, I am not having second thoughts. I would just like to read the book for myself since I got caught up in its net as well," she exclaimed.

A day or two later, she met the handsome, young, sea captain Tony Frenic. Buffett's book might have been the Holy Grail to Bubba but one look at Captain Frenic and Sherry forgot all about the book.

She reasoned in her excitement that the book of short stories had been pushed under the sofa. It was a perfect plausible story, but could there be another reason just as plausible. She had to think that maybe it was Bubba reaching out to her. His way of telling her he was alright.

She curled up on the couch and began to read the first story. "Take Another Road" was the story Bubba had always talked about. She understood why after only reading a few pages. The story read like a road map of the last five years of their lives. Like her Bubba before her, she was fast asleep in no time at all, no doubt dreaming about Tully Mars and his horse Mr. Twain.

TWO ISLANDS; ONE STORY

Chapter 6

A slight breeze blew off the sea and into her face. She was walking down a snow-white beach barefooted. Her blonde hair neatly framed her beautiful face. A white morning dress flowed in the ocean's breeze. It was hard to realize that the woman walking down the beach was, in fact. her but in a brief moment, Sherry saw the face of the lady and it was her own.

A mile out to sea, she saw a sailboat coming toward her. She knew there was something special, almost familiar about the craft. She then saw him just beyond the reef. "Is it you, is it you, Bubba Lee?" she heard herself call out.

A massive four-legged creature joined the man on the boat's deck. "It was - yes it was Jester. The man had to be Bubba Lee." Once again she heard her own voice. The man on the deck of the sailboat turned to face her. It was the one her heart missed the most, it was Bubba Lee and she saw him wave when he saw her.

"Sherry, Sherry, are you in there?" a voice called out and shattered the scene. She awoke from her dream and looked at the clock on the wall. "Sherry, Sherry," she heard again, along with a rap on her door.

"It's three in the morning, this better be good," she thought to herself. She then remembered through her sleep and the wine that Bubba was still missing. She jumped to her feet and ran to the door thinking it might be news of Bubba.

It wasn't news about the missing cowboy that surprised her when she opened the door but she was surprised nonetheless. Captain Frenic was on the other side of the door. He was the last person, besides Bubba, that she expected to see that night.

"I'm sorry sweetheart, I would have been here sooner but it proved harder than I thought to get a flight out of Buenos Aires. I got the message from Jon that Bubba was missing while docked in Montevideo. I tried calling you but it seems like people could call in but no one could call out," Frenic explained.

"Wait a minute, who called you?" she asked through sleepy eyes.

"Jon, Jon Carpenter," he answered, thinking she was aware of the call. "Are you going to question me all morning out here on the porch?" was his next question.

"I'm sorry Tony. You just woke me from a dead sleep. Come on in, I'll fix some coffee and catch you up to speed before I go to work," she told him.

She went back to the beginning as she fixed the coffee. Sherry started with the little spat she and Bubba got into the day Captain Tony shipped out. He was amazed to find Bubba Lee was jealous of him and admitted he was a little jealous of Bubba.

"You men are worse than women," said Sherry, "Now why would you be jealous of him. That makes about as much sense as him being jealous of you." She found neither credible.

"Well Sherry, for starters, he knows you, like I wish I knew you. You two have so much history together. I'll never know you as a little girl; I wasn't there when you learned to drive or when you graduated from college. Bubba was there for all of that," Tony confessed.

"That is so sweet. Stupid, but sweet," she said before kissing him.

"There is something else about him," Captain Tony said out loud. "He has that childlike spirit of adventure. To me this is just my job. Every time

Bubba goes out, it's an adventure to him. I am envious of Bubba most of all because he's not afraid to dream."

"We are all envious of that," she added after taking in Frenic's words. She saw a different side of both of the men she loved in the wee hours of the morning. She saw a side of Tony she had never seen before and she saw a side of Bubba she had long since forgotten.

The days that followed went slowly by for all those who waited to hear the fate of the missing cowboy and his dog. Sherry's high spirits and positive outlook began to wane. It didn't help that no words of encouragement seemed to be forthcoming from the Coast Guard station. There was little to no news to be exact but the cutters were still at sea. The island's only hope was hanging on that one fact.

Jon Carpenter was beginning to look twice his age. The self-proclaimed playboy of St. Renee had taken himself out of the game. His days were spent running back and forth between the Yellow Rose and the Coast Guard station. Bubba's first mate had been reduced to a carrier of no news.

Captain Tony's boat had returned from its voyage but it would soon set sail again. It proved to be the hardest thing he had ever done, leaving Sherry in such despair. She understood that an unemployed

155

sea Captain wouldn't do anyone any good. She helped push him to return to his ship. The only request she made was that while he was at sea, he keep a lookout for Bubba.

Doc had been a God send; he was one of the reasons Frenic felt comfortable about returning to the sea. The writer watched over Sherry like a hawk. What bit of news that Carpenter brought from the authorities had to be filtered through Doc. Jon Carpenter, in a lot of ways, was just a crusty old sea dog, who never learned how to ease into a conversation. He was good as gold, but at times too blunt.

Sherry and her three Musketeers were not the only ones on edge. The whole village seemed to be on pins and needles. They had grown fond of their adopted Texans. It seemed like more and more fear gripped the small island. Each day the people got a little closer believing that the worst had happened to the crew of the Texas Ship of Fools. The once-happy little village had grown silent.

The day came when Captain Tony was due to ship out. Sherry hid her emotions as she walked him to the docks. She knew if her true feeling were known, Frenic would sacrifice all he had worked for.

"Sherry, you just say the word and I'll stay," he said when they reached his ship.

"No, I'll be fine. I've got lots of help. You just hurry back, every chance you get, and if you see Bubba, tell him to get his butt home," she said, speaking in a way that only a woman from Texas could.

"Will do Ma'am! See Doc has been teaching a little Texan, here and there," Captain Tony bragged.

She laughed and kissed him goodbye. It would be a month before they saw one another again, so the kiss was long and deep. She waved once more as her Captain made his way to the bridge. The tugs were already waiting to escort the ship out to sea. One final look from the lovers and then their moment would become a memory.

Sherry found a visitor waiting for her when she returned to the Yellow Rose. In the booth where Bubba Lee used to sit was Captain Boulet. "I came as soon as the news reached me," the Captain reported to her. "Has there been any news about my boy?" Boulet wanted to know.

She was just about to fill the Captain in when Jon Carpenter came running through the door. "They're back, The Coast Guard's boats are coming up the channel," he conveyed to anyone who could hear him.

Everyone in the Yellow Rose ran to the docks. The news spread like wild fire through the village and soon almost everyone in town was gathered at the docks in the harbor. The Coast Guard cutter made her way up the channel to the ever-growing crowd. In the front row of the people gathered stood Sherry, Doc, Carpenter, and Captain Boulet.

Every heart pounded as they watched the crew of the cutter man their stations and bring her to rest in her slip. The Captain soon appeared at the top of the gang plank. The grim look he wore read like a cheap novel. It might have been the first time in twenty years of service, he wished for a different vocation.

Everyone could tell the news wasn't good just by the expression on the Coast Guard Captain's face. The Captain walked past the crowd to where Sherry and her three friends were. Doc put his arm around her as the Captain began to speak.

"I'm so sorry; we have turned the waters inside out. It's like the sea swallowed up the Texas Ship of Fools and her crew. We looked everywhere and there was no sign....." the man would have continued but Sherry fainted into Doc's arms.

"Quick, let's get her back up to the Yellow Rose," Carpenter said as he lifted her limp body. "Someone get a doctor."

A few people turned to the man who had the word (Doc) on his belt buckle. "Sorry, I am not that kind of doctor. For God's sake, someone get a real doctor," Sherry's old friend and history professor exclaimed.

They placed her in a booth once they got her back to the café. Doc went to get her something to drink while Carpenter ran everyone but Boulet out of the Yellow Rose. No one said a word; no one knew exactly where to start.

Finally Boulet broke the silence, "Damn those land lovers, sons-a-bitches would be lucky to find their own ass and that's using two hands. Jon, let's go find the boy and get him home where he belongs and the mutt too. There are a thousand islands out there and I know every single one like a mother knows her child.

Sherry, you have to help. You can do that by being strong, for yourself and for Bubba. I don't care what they tell you; unless you see his body, you always give him the benefit of the doubt. Child, can you do that?" said Boulet, speaking with a Cajun flavor. One could always tell when he was upset, 'cause that's when the French Creole in him came out the most.

She shook her head 'yes' through her tears. "You bring my Bubba Lee back," she told him before he left for the docks.

"I'll get my gear and be down there directly, Captain," Carpenter called after Boulet.

The island's doctor came in the front door just as Boulet was leaving. Carpenter saw it as a chance to talk to Doc before meeting up with Captain Boulet.

"Doc, years ago in another time zone, as well as another life, I gave my word to Bubba that I would be there for Sherry if something happened to him. I am leaving her in your hands," said Carpenter, finishing his little speech.

"We'll be fine, you just got to get Bubba," was the writer's only request.

"Remember Sherry, no giving up," he said to her before leaving.

Carpenter and Boulet had been on the hunt for a week, stopping at every small island that dotted the Caribbean Sea. Those who they spoke to knew of the famous story-telling Cowboy, but no one had seen him, his dog or the boat.

Carpenter was beginning to lose faith he'd ever see his old friend again. Boulet, on the other hand, would not lose the faith. He had been to the edge and should have died more than once. The good Lord never gave up on him and he wasn't about to give up on Bubba. Boulet would not give up, not without proof in one form or the other. He could not go back without something; not after the promises he had made to Sherry.

The second week of their search took them to a small island a hundred miles south of Jamaica. Boulet had gone into the village for supplies and do some asking around. It was the same routine that had followed since leaving St Renee. Sometimes depending on their timing, they would stop twice a day.

Carpenter was on the verge of losing it; he couldn't take another letdown. It was coming up on a month since Bubba had disappeared into the hurricane. Each day he heard the same answer, always "no," no one had run across a stray cowboy and oversized dog. He told Boulet he'd stay with the boat; he just couldn't bear to hear another "no."

He sat on the deck in a rickety old lawn chair for nearly an hour with his thoughts. He found the alone time wasn't helping his state of mind either. He decided a walk down the beach. It might clear the negativity out of his head. Boulet would be in the village for a few more hours so Carpenter knew he would not be missed.

161

His thoughts turned to Bubba Lee as he walked along the shore line. He had so many memories of his friend and they were as clear as the day they occurred. His first memory was him as a buck private in a world lost to time.

Sergeant McBride called him his Yankee Boy. In the beginning of his tour, he hated Bubba. Sergeant McBride rode his ass constantly. It was Yankee Boy this, Yankee Boy that. But in the end, all of Bubba's needling kept Carpenter alive.

Both men then were rotated back to the states. It should have been the end of the relationship because they had very little in common. Bubba was a snuff-dipping cowboy from Texas, while Carpenter was a skirt-chasing deckhand from Michigan.

Every time Jon Carpenter found his ass in a crack, it was Bubba he called, just like in Nam. The first time Bubba flew all the way to Flint to bail his Yankee Boy out of jail, Carpenter said, "I swear Bubba, I had no idea she was the judge's daughter." It was still funny remembering his words.

It was late-night phone calls, laced with drunken rants and broken-hearted stories. Still after all that, Bubba thought enough of him to make him his first mate.

162

Carpenter was looking back at his memories and not paying much attention to what was ahead of him. He suddenly tripped over an object and fell face first into the sand. "What the…," he said, looking back for what had caused his fall.

It was a board, three-and-a-half feet long, sticking out of the sand. He saw that the piece of wood was charred around the edges. He picked it up to throw it out of the way so another idiot would repeat the wreck. But Carpenter stopped dead in his tracks when he saw the black lettering on one side. It was only one word, but that was all it took. The word was "Fools" and he knew it well because he was the one that painted it on the side of Bubba's boat.

The board with the single word printed on it dropped the man to his knees. It was like a three-hundred-pound man had jumped on his chest. He had been on the edge all morning but the relic gave him the final shove. Tears began to stream down the hardened man's face.

"Damn you Bubba Lee, you son of a bitch, don't do this shit to me," he repeated over and over.

The man noticed through his tears something black laying in the weeds. He held his breath as he walked over to it. Carpenter bent down to find it was a hat. Not just any hat; it was the very same hat everybody saw when they looked at Bubba Lee. He turned the hat over just to make sure. "Custom made for Bubba McBride by Mike's Hatters," was printed on the hat's sweat band.

The hat was like everything else in Bubba's life, it had a story. One year Bubba had taken Sherry to the Fort Worth Stock Show. He was looking and she was shopping. He said both were about to wear him out.

He then ran on to a couple of old friends: Chuck and Mike. Now these two gents were as different as you could find. Chuck was a small man, while his running buddy was as big as any bull entered in the rodeo. The truth was the little guy was the tough one. Mike was like a big, old, lovable teddy bear.

They told Bubba of a card game going on in the back of someone's horse trailer. Bubba excused himself from his job of following Sherry around like a pack mule and he and the boys went to find the game. Bubba took their money and won a new custom-made hat in the process.

Carpenter sank in the sand, drained of hope and in tears. Bubba and Jester were gone, it was unbearable to think of, but he held the proof in his hands. Nothing seemed to move around the man. He heard nothing, he saw nothing but he felt the pain. That was the only sense he seemed to have left. He finally just went numb, clinging to the old cowboy hat.

Carpenter heard something behind him, but the sounds felt like what he might have heard in a dream. The man was so in tune with his grief that whatever seemed to be going on around him was a blur. All at once a voice invaded his thoughts.

"Jon, Jon, boy can't you hear me? I've been looking all over for you." He looked up to find Boulet standing over him.

It was like he had gone mute. He looked up at Boulet but could not speak. He gently handed the Captain what he had found, the last remains of their friend. It was Boulet's turn to go silent as he looked over the hat and piece of the Texas Ship of Fools. It was true: they just knew the cowboy and Jester were lost to him but it meant so much more to Boulet.

The boat that saved Boulet's life a quarter of a century ago was also lost. Thoughts began to flood into his mind. The "what if's" men sometimes ask themselves, like, "If I'd never sold the cowboy the boat, they'd both would still be afloat," or "Maybe if I'd have trained him better, perhaps that was the answer."

The two men sat side by side on the beach, each lost in the grief. Hours passed and they were still there. "Bubba was special; hell I never have gotten close to anyone like I did him," said Boulet, breaking the silence.

"I know what you mean. I was married three times. I told him things I wouldn't tell anyone," said Carpenter agreeing with Boulet.

The two men stayed a little while longer before heading back to the Deliverance. Once back aboard, they hoisted their anchor and started back.

It was late in the afternoon when the Deliverance sailed into port. The port master put the boat right beside the slip where The Texas Ship of Fools used to be. Carpenter shook his head. "This ain't going to be easy, is it?" he asked.

"Nope, it might be the hardest thing I've ever done. Believe me, I've done some hard shit in my day; this will be it for me," Boulet said. But Carpenter wouldn't come to understand the full scope what his friend was trying to say later.

They tied the boat off and grabbed the hat and the piece of wood they had found. They were all ready to get the deal over with when a man told them Sherry and Doc had gone to the mainland; something about a horse.

"Damn it, I forgot all about the horse," Carpenter said out loud.

"What horse?" the Captain asked.

"About six months ago, Sherry asked me to go back to Texas with her. I asked her why and she said she had to go pick out Bubba's Birthday present. I figured she was talking about a pair of boots or something. She didn't tell me, until we drove up to Chubby Turner's place, that she was going to buy Bubba a freaking horse. She had bought some pasture land just west of the village for the animal. Why she asked me to go, I'll never know. You can put everything I know about a horse in three or four words. I just let the delivery date slip my mind; it's not like I didn't have anything else to worry about," he said, filling the Captain in.

"Now what?" Boulet wanted to know.

"Now we wait. I don't know about you, but I need a drink. I've needed one for some time. I know you don't drink, but I'd appreciate the company," Carpenter told Boulet.

Carpenter walked right past the wait staff at the Yellow Rose, past the dining area and directly to the bar. He reached behind the bar and got a fresh bottle of Jack. He returned to Bubba's booth with the bottle in hand

By then, all eyes were on Carpenter. The waitress knew the man, in fact she had shared her bed with him more than once but she had never seen him in such a state. She started to say something to him but Boulet stopped her.

Carpenter then asked that the Cowboy's mason jar be filled with ice tea and Jester's bowl be brought from the kitchen. All watched as the ritual played itself out before their eyes. The man cracked the seal on the whisky bottle and poured himself a shot and then another and another. He began to speak after his third belt.

"I drink to the memory of my Sergeant, the man who brought most of his boys home from the war and the man who kicked Charlie's ass more times than not. This is to Sergeant McBride." Carpenter threw a shot down.

"I drink to my friend, the man who was always there in good times and bad; a man who never turned another man away." He downed the second shot.

"I drink to my Captain, the mutt and the Texas Ship of Fools, fair weather and calm seas Bubba Lee." He downed the last shot with a single tear running down his face, turned the glass upside down and slammed it to the table.

"Now my friends, if you do not mind, I'd like to get drunk alone," he said to the crowd.

The Yellow Rose fell silent as the island folk began to file out. Each left with a heavy heart; the cowboy and his dog would be dearly missed. Carpenter sat alone at the table with his bottle, saying goodbye the only way he knew.

Boulet was stuck in a holding pattern; he did not want to impose on his friend's grief and he did not want to answer a lot of questions by the people outside. He thought he'd go through the kitchen and duck out the back door.

Boulet found a surprise waiting behind the double kitchen doors. She sat at the butcher block in tears.

"How much of that story did you hear, child?" the old Captain questioned.

"Enough. Enough to know Bubba's gone. Take me to him, let me tell him goodbye, I beg of you," Sherry pleaded.

The old Captain had trouble forcing his next words out. "I can't; we didn't find a body. We found a badly burned piece of his boat and his cowboy hat," he reported.

"Then there's a chance he might still be out there?" Sherry asked with hope in her eyes.

"Calm down child and hear me now. Men such as your Bubba are very rare. They leave no trace when they depart for the hereafter. You see, men like Bubba Lee McBride never die; they are immortal. They live through the ages in the stories told about them. They live in the hearts of those they left behind. Whether he's dead or alive, you will never lose Bubba, he's in your heart.

"No child, I cannot tell you Bubba's dead, only God has that answer. Who knows, maybe someday the doors will fly open and Bubba Lee will walk through them with a new batch of stories. Until that day, he and his old mutt lives within your heart," Boulet said before he made his exit.

The old Captain found Doc and Jim Moore at the docks; they had just heard the news. It wasn't hard to see the writer was shaken.

"Moore, what would you charge to carry an old fool home?" Boulet wanted to know.

"I don't know, what about the Deliverance," he asked, curious why the old Captain was leaving his boat.

"I'm done with it, done with it all. Doc, you tell Sherry it's hers to save until the day the doors fly open. She'll know what I mean," Boulet stated in a tired voice

Two weeks before his friends had found the remains of his boat and the morning after Bubba had heard the words of Gordon Maatsch, his eyes opened. He had a feeling something was different. He rolled over and there was no Jester. The man rose straight up in a moment of fear. He looked at the other end of the small raft and still his dog was nowhere in sight. Suddenly he heard the playful sounds of his pooch. Bubba turned his head to find the dog running up and down a stretch of shore.

Had they really found land or had the good Lord taken them in the night. He halfway expected to see his old foreman come riding out of the tree line.

"My Lord son, you gonna sleep all day. Didn't I teach you better?" he imagined what Maatsch might say.

It was not heaven they had found and he and Jester were still very much among the living. His dingy and his island of inflatable rafts had come to rest on a reef. A hundred feet beyond the reef was the shore and Jester running back and forth.

Bubba Lee jumped out of the nineteenth century dingy to find the water was shallow. He deduced from it that it was low tide. He rocked his raft until he broke her and her tagalongs free. He pulled them one by one to the shore where he was met by his four-legged companion.

It wasn't hard to see that the dog was excited. Bubba, himself, felt like dancing a jig. He knew by the time he had everything ashore, Jester had claimed the island in the way male dogs mark their territory. Bubba had a gut-laugh, he hadn't had one of those in some time.

"Permission to come ashore almighty Canine, King Pooch, Lord Mutt" he joked with Jester.

The man sat down to catch his breath after getting the last raft on dry land. Questions by the score hit him as he rested. Questions like: "Where was he?" "Were there people on the island?" and, more importantly, "Were they friendly?" One thing he knew to be certain, "It was good to be out of the dingy and on dry land."

Bubba thought it might be a good idea to find a place to stash his things after he rested a bit. He found a place where the brush was thick beyond the sandy beach. It was a good two-hour chore to put everything away, but it felt good to move around freely. The one item he took with him was his rifle and pistol.

"Come on boy, let's see if we can't find us some fresh breakfast," he said, calling to the dog.

Bubba had seen thicker jungles, but not in some time. It seemed like he had to hack his way through

172

the biggest part of it. Man had left no sign, not as far as he could tell. He did see some wild boar tracks and took it as a good omen.

Fresh game meant fresh water and barring any cannibals lurking in the tall grass, they'd be fine, even without people. They came to a clearing after about an hour of trailblazing. A deep cool stream ran through the middle of it.

Banana trees as well as coconut trees were everywhere. He grabbed the closest batch and peeled a banana for himself, then another for Jester. Prime rib couldn't have tasted much better, not to the man anyway. Jester, on the other hand, seemed to balk at first but managed to get the thing eaten.

Bubba washed his breakfast down with a drink from the stream. The water was cold and sweet; he couldn't help but take a second drink. A thought hit him. If the water tasted that good, what would it feel like. He skinned off the clothes he'd had on for going on a week. Buck naked and not giving a damn, he dived in. Jester was not that far behind.

The experience took him back to his last days on the ranch. The summer had been downright hell-like. No rain, no wind, just triple-digit temperatures on a daily basis. Bubba was gathering strays when he ran across a natural spring. It didn't take him long to jump in that day either.

They headed back to the beach after their brunch and bath. His swim that morning had given him a new idea. It might be better to walk around the island rather than through it. His reasoning was two-fold; his first reason was it would be a way to get an idea how big the land mass was; the second was he knew populations congregated closer to shore.

The three-hour-old explorer put together a backpack once he returned to his stash. He packed enough supplies for a few days. He broke down his rod and reel and tied it to the bottom of the knapsack.

"Come on boy, it's time for a road trip. Well on second thought, I'm looking for a road, trip," he said with a laugh.

It was late in the afternoon when the leader of the McBride party stopped. He could gauge by the position of the sun, they were nearing the other side of the island. He could have pushed on, but he still had a shelter to build and supper to catch.

He'd guessed he had walked seven to eight miles. He had yet to see any sign of life and was fearful they had been dumped on a deserted piece of Atlantic real estate. He might have been discouraged if it wasn't for the days spent adrift.

They had a much better chance on land than they did on water.

The next morning they awoke refreshed and eager to continue on their journey. Bubba slung his pack on his shoulder before picking up his rifle.

"Let's go Jester," he hollered at his fellow castaway who was busy marking more territory.

Within an hour, Bubba saw his first sign of man and it was not what he had hoped. The beach ahead of him looked like a graveyard of past storms. At first glance, he took note of three to four wrecks. He guessed the oldest was at least two-hundred years old. One looked to be what was left of a German U-boat, maybe from WWI. The rest, the Texas cowboy didn't have a clue.

"Where the hell are we, the freaking Hades," he mumbled to himself.

Bubba's first thought was to get the hell out of Dodge. He was a firm believer in ghosts; he had run across a few in his lifetime. Two nights earlier, he had heard the voice of his first foreman in his head; who's to say it wasn't Maatsch's ghost.

He thought it through and decided it would be in his best interesst to have a quick look around. He knew he might learn something or find something that would aid in his survival.

What do you say Jester? he asked his dog as he dropped his pack. "Are you up to a little recon?"

In the belly of an old tall ship, he found some Spanish helmets and in one, the skull of the previous owner was still encased. The boat was older than he first thought. Bubba could tell by the artifacts he was finding that perhaps it was twice as old. He also found a number of items he could use if he had to.

He didn't find any treasure but what the hell was he going to do with pirate booty? It wasn't like he could run down to the local 7-Eleven for a slurpy.

Bubba thought he'd make a mental note and return at a later date after he had a better idea of what his needs were. He went through the other wrecks with the same reasoning in mind. He did pick up an old German Luger he found on the U-boat's wreckage. He doubted it would fire but it would be fun to play with.

He was about to begin his journey again when he noticed an ancient path. He figured he would see where it led before he continued. "Come on boy, let's see where this goes," he said to Jester with a bit of excitement in his voice.

The veteran of the Vietnam War had been trained in survival skills and he had first-hand knowledge of surviving in the jungle. All he had been taught came back in no time at all. The first thing he was taught was how to watch for and read signs. He hadn't seen any evidence of living human life since he had been on the island but he knew some could be lying in wait.

The path looked as old as time itself: overgrown without signs of use. It led into the heart of the island - some one-thousand yards. It made a circle through a stream and then up a mountainside. Bubba found a pretty good-sized cave over halfway up. He could tell by the number of old, rusted-out tin cans at its opening that there had been people there at one time.

He dropped his pack again and then rummaged through it until he was holding his flash light. Bubba slowly but surely made his way through the sheets of spider webs until he came to what appeared to be a large room. He began by shining his light in a 360-degree pattern.

Three skeletal remains startled him at first. On further inspection, he knew he had found what was left of the crew of the U-boat. Bubba was no detective but it wasn't too hard to put the picture together of what had happened. It appeared that the ranking officer had killed his men and then turned his own cold hand on himself.

What was the reason for the murder suicide? That was the real mystery. He saw wooden crates of c-rations piled in one corner, and amo boxes in the other. They didn't starve; that was almost a fact. The only thing he could think of was they went crazy. It was pretty easy to come to that conclusion because the German officer still held the pistol.

"Damn boy, let's get out of here, we can come back later to visit. Now you all don't get up, we can find our way out," Bubba said to the skeletal remains, halfway kidding.

Bubba could have gone back to the beach and continued his walk around the island but he decided to go to the top of the mountain instead. He figured he might be able to see the entire island from that vantage point. They climbed higher and higher until they reached the summit.

He stood like a conquering hero on the top of the mountain. The view was simply breathtaking from that elevation. He could see a panoramic layout of the whole island from where he and Jester stood. The place where he and his dog had washed to shore looked to be some ten miles in length. The land mass was long but it was no more than two miles across. He could go from side to side in a

178

matter of minutes if the right trails were cut through the jungle. His mind was thinking like a finely tuned instrument.

He had seen spools of cable on one of the wrecks and he thought there might be enough to build a zip line. He could travel across the island in less time then. "Hell we're here anyway, we might as well be industrious," he said to no one in particular.

He then made the choice to go down the other side of the mountain. He reasoned he would then be back to the spot where he had stashed his belongings. He could also mark the trail on the way back.

The way back felt a little different. Unlike his walk down the beach, he had a feeling he and Jester were not alone. He shrugged it off as being in the dingy too long or the ghosts of the German soldiers he had seen in the cave. More than likely, from the number of wrecks he'd seen, there were probably a whole host of ghosts on the island. His only prayer was not to become one of them.

He had a pretty good idea how the island was laid out by the time he reached the beach and where he and his dog had washed up. It seemed reasonable that he and Jester, with the exception a few ghosts, were alone. He also knew after barely two days on the island that there was no way to be sure. He slept lightly like he had done the night before, with his hand on his gun.

Let's get a good night's rest and we'll hit it hard first thing in the morning," Bubba said out loud.

He had been missing for seven months but it didn't seem nearly as long. Every day was filled with work and it made the time go faster. He knew by then, no one was looking for the two castaways; it was a hard pill to swallow. He and Jester were alive and that had to count for something. But it was up to him to get rescued and by then everyone must have been thinking the worst.

His mind would always go to Sherry whenever he let it wander. He could only imagine what she was going through. The worst part about it was he had no way to make it stop. The only thing he could do was try to get found as soon as possible. The letters he wrote to her in his head were multiplying, but they kept him from going crazy.

His first three months on the island were spent cutting brush and piling it into bonfires all along the beach. The next thing on his to-do list was to haul brush up to the mountain top.

In the cave where he had found the remains of the German soldiers, he later found two cases of French wine. Bubba had been on the wagon for years, but he still found use for the wine. He would use it to prime the fires if and when he saw a boat or a plane. A few of the bottles were used to send real letters to Sherry, just like he did the first day he was adrift.

The last few months he busied himself first with the zip line and then a hut by the stream where he and Jester had their first breakfast as the only known citizens of the island. All he needed was the professor and he'd be up there with the most famous castaways of all.

SECRETS REVEALED

Chapter 7

Bubba had nearly gained Sainthood in the year he had been gone. Stories were told and songs had been written about the legendary Captain Cowboy and his faithful dog. He had become the Texas version of the Jolly Man, (a mythical minstrel made famous in a Buffett tune and later a children's book).

There were at least two or three sightings of him a month. He was seen at a football game in Joe Robby Stadium when the Miami Dolphins played the Dallas Cowboys. Another time, he was helping the DEA round up cartel kingpins in South America. In the end not even Elvis got around like Captain Cowboy.

Sherry was shaken in the beginning when the sightings were halfway believable. She'd get her hopes up only to have them shot down. One day Carpenter stepped in, telling her if Bubba was out there, he'd turn over heaven or hell to get to her if he could. She did stop letting the sightings get to her but she never gave up hope that one day Bubba Lee would return.

Jon Carpenter thought enough time had passed to have a conversation with Sherry and one night he came a calling.

"Sherry, I know this is hard to hear, hell it's hard for me to say," said Carpenter. "We're gonna have to have some kind of memorial service for Bubba. It doesn't mean you or I have to give up hope but it seems like the right thing to do. These people and his friends everywhere - he did get around - need closure. It would mean a lot and maybe put some of these rumors to bed." She listened as he talked.

"It might sound funny coming from me, one of the last true believers, but I've been thinking the same thing," said Sherry. "We could have what you are thinking about but I would much rather have a celebration; a party Bubba Lee would be pissed that he missed. Even if the worst is true, he had much rather us celebrate his and Jester's lives than mourn over them.

"I have been making plans, and have ordered something real special for the occasion. We'll have what you and everyone else wants to have as soon as it arrives," she said, answering his concerns.

Carpenter had already said he goodbyes when someone knocked on her front door. "It's a regular Grand Central Station around here tonight," she told him.

Doc had chosen to stay on the island after Bubba's disappearance and Sherry had asked him if he'd write a book about the missing cowboy and his dog. She even offered him Bubba's little house as a place to stay. The truth was, she got used to having him around because he was so much like Bubba. It was Doc that night at the door, and he was wearing a serious look upon his face.

"Good I'm glad I found both of you together," he said. Both Sherry and Jon Carpenter knew there was something wrong just by the way the writer looked. She asked Doc to come in, sit down and tell them what was on his mind that bothered him so. He took a deep breath and then began to speak.

"Today I was cleaning in the closet in the front room of Bubba's house when I found a smell metal box with his papers. I wasn't going to open it but there was a note on top that said to do so. I found two letters inside: one from your mother, Sherry, and a short one from Bubba. I will read them out loud if you like." She agreed and he began to read the letter from her mother first.

"Dear Bubba Lee,

Bubba, you know you were always like a son to John and I, and we loved you as such. John has gone on and I will be joining him soon. I cannot go until I reveal a secret that I've held on to for over thirty years.

John and I stood up for your mom and dad when they were married;, they were our best friends. I was there the night you came kicking and screaming into the world, those may have been the last tears anyone ever saw you cry. We knew from day one a cowboy was born.

What few know was years later your mother had a second child, a baby girl. I was there for her birth as well. It was hard bringing your little sister into the world, and a few hours later your mother died.

Your dad was heartbroken, his spirit had been shattered. He had a ranch to run, a son to raise and a newborn to nurture. It was too much for him and he knew it. He knew John and I couldn't have children and so he gave us the most wonderful gift: your sister. We named her Sherry after your mother.

When your dad died, we tried to get you to join your sister but you had too much McBride in you. There was no getting you off the ranch.

We intended to tell both of you the truth but never got around to it. It was our biggest mistake; I know that now. To watch you and Sherry, no one would know you weren't brother and sister.

185

Bubba, I know I should tell her myself and I would if there was more time. I didn't want to go to my grave with this secret. It's hard enough to bear that we've lied to you two all these many years.

I realize it's not fair of me to ask, but would you tell her for me. As I said, my time is short. You both have grown into very special people and I love you very much.

Mom

Sherry was in tears by the time Doc finished the first letter. Jon Carpenter put his arm around her to comfort her.

"My big brother is gone, he's really gone," was all she could say with tears streaming down her face.

"Perhaps it would be better if you read Bubba's letter in private," Doc suggested and she agreed. Later that night, Carpenter told Doc he was glad because he didn't think he could sit through another such tear jerker.

Sherry would wait before reading Bubba's last words. Like her two friends, she could only handle so much emotionally. Her mother had left her a lot to sort through. She also had to ask herself why Bubba had never said anything.

Her memory took her back to that last night with Bubba; the fight they had, and, yes, an almost slip of his tongue. He almost told her the truth that night and she didn't even notice.

The morning after hearing the true origin of her birth, she opened the second letter over a cup of coffee. It was not as long as her mother's but it was classic Bubba Lee.

Dearest Sherry,

Hey girl, if you are reading this, it means I hung'em up. Don't be sad, 'cause I had one hell of a run. The best part of it was you. The good Lord only knows where I'd be if not for your nipping at my heels. You don't have to worry, hell by the time you read this, Old Strings Dijon is probably talking my ear off.

I guess you've read your mother's letter by now. Please don't be hard on her; she loved you more than anything. I would have told you but what difference would it have made. I think deep down you and I always knew the truth. Since day one, in our hearts, and now in reality, we were always brother and sister.

Well I guess I better go now, I've got a long trail to ride through the tall and the uncut. Alright, alright, I'm coming Strings.

I'll tell our parents hi, for you. One more thing girl: smile.

Love, Bubba

Sherry began to speak out loud to Bubba, as though he was right there. "Alright big brother, if you want a smile I'll give you one. It doesn't mean that I am giving up on your coming home. The one thing I can't do for you is give up hope. Sorry big brother," she vowed.

During the weeks that followed, Sherry began acting very secretive. She had hired a manager to take over her duties at the Yellow Rose because she was hardly ever there. She was always on the phone or in a meeting when she was there. She had made three separate trips back to Texas without explanation.

The new in-thing for Carpenter and Doc to do was sit around trying to figure out what she was up to; all the close meetings and not being able to get a straight answer was driving them nuts. Heaven forbid, when one of them cornered her long enough to ask what she was up to.

"Patience boys, you'll know soon enough," was her standard answer.

They could see whatever she was up to was bringing her great joy, so they didn't push the issue. It had something to do with her brother, whatever it was. Carpenter had made the comment, "Bubba acted like that when he was fixing to spring something," he told Doc.

"At least we know she comes by it honestly," was Doc's reply

It was damn sure catching her in whatever she was up to. And Doc had pulled a disappearing act on Carpenter. Every morning they took their coffee together. One morning Doc was there like any other day and the next morning he was gone. Carpenter was feeling like the lost relative, twice removed.

It had gotten so lonely for Carpenter that he was waiting at the docks when Captain Franic made port. They had become pretty good friends over that year. In fact, he had even gone to sea with the Captain a few times.

Frenic and Sherry were still pretty much an item, or at least they were until she went all black-outs on everyone. Captain Frenic was usually there with Carpenter and Doc drinking coffee when he was in port. Frenic was just as much in the dark as Carpenter when it came to what his girlfriend was up to.

That was one of the reasons why Jon Carpenter was waiting at the docks for his friend. He felt they shared that one thing in common, neither one of them knew what the hell she was up to.

"Man, I am glad to see you Captain," Carpenter said one morning while grinning ear to ear. Frenic stopped long enough for a quick hand shake.

"I wish I had time to talk Jon, but Sherry said she needed to see me ASAP," Frenic said, trying to explain.

Carpenter just stood there dumbfounded, his smile slowly disappearing. "Is everybody going crazy or is it me," he had to ask himself as he watched Captain Frenic walk away.

The more he thought about it, the madder he found himself. But who the hell was he going to get mad at? All his friends were disappearing. He had taken all the closed-door meetings and secret talks he was going to take. He was going to get to the bottom of the madness - whatever it took.

"Wait a damn minute Captain, I am going with you," Carpenter yelled to Frenic. "I am sorry Captain, but damn it, I'm tired of being in the dark," he told Frenic when he caught up with him.

"I don't know what to tell you, Jon. All I know is I got a telegram saying she needed to see me as soon as I made port," said Captain Frenic, trying his best to explain to his slightly irritated friend.

"Well I am going with you. I am sick of being the red-headed stepchild," said Carpenter, asserted himself.

"Suit yourself, it's your neck," Frenic snapped back.

Carpenter was beginning to question his hasty behavior by the time they reached her door. The last thing he wanted to do was get her angry. He had seen her mad before and it was not a pretty sight. He held his breath and expected the worse when Frenic knocked on the door.

She was in a cheerful mood and happy to see both men, much to Carpenter's dismay.

"I was just fixing to send for you, Jon," she said after kissing her boyfriend. "Well you come in; we have a lot to go over," Sherry said, extending an invitation.

The men had somewhat of a dumbfounded look on his face. If her words were any sweeter, they'd be dripping with honey. She disappeared into the kitchen and then came back with a beer for both men. Carpenter could only watch with utter amazement.

"Well, let's get to it," she said with a handful of papers. That proved to be the tipping point for Carpenter.

"Get to what Sherry? If you did notice, I'm the one in the dark. I used to have company in there with Doc but now even he has disappeared. I wish someone would clue me in, "the frustrated man exclaimed.

"Well Jon, it's been a bit of a secret I have been working on. I wanted to make sure I was able to pull it off before involving many people. You remember when you and I talked about doing something for Bubba and Jester? Jon, that's what I have been working on: a celebration for him and Jester.

"I sent Doc to Texas to get some of Bubba's favorite singers for the entertainment. That's one reason why I wanted to speak to you. Is the Deliverance up to a trip to Miami to pick up Doc and the singers he's secured?" she asked.

"She's fine," responded a surprised Doc. "We just got the new cooler installed last week. That reminds me, why did the Deliverance need a walk-in freezer?"

"Not only do I need to pick up the singers but I also need a thousand pounds of beef that I've ordered for this little shindig," she informed him.

"I can't sail her by myself, I'm going to need one other person," Carpenter explained.

"Tony will go with you, won't you darling," she said, like he had a choice.

"And it would be a pleasure to serve under my esteemed Captain Jon," Frenic said, finally speaking up.

"This is rich," Carpenter added when he heard the name of his crew.

Four days later, Carpenter was sailing the Deliverance into the Port of Miami. He saw Doc waiting with three other men carrying guitar cases. Later he would learn their names: Brian Burns, Larry Joe Taylor, and Tommy Alverson.

"Man I am glad to see you, Jon. It was hard work rounding up all this entertainment. I tell you Jon, it's like herding cats," Doc said jokingly.

The Deliverance set sail for Saint Renee shortly after the singers and Sherry's beef was loaded. It was a good voyage back with the entertainers pitching in when needed and they were handy with a song.

Carpenter understood why Sherry had settled on the three. Each one was a reminder of a different side of Bubba Lee. Alverson was about the best he ever heard when it came down to honky-tonk, beer-drinking music. Larry Joe was the closest thing to having Jimmy Buffett without having Jimmy Buffett.

Brian Burns had to be Carpenter's favorite, for the mere fact that he sang, "The Wreck of the Edmond Fitzgerald" better than Gordon Lightfoot. Not only could Burns sing the song but he knew the names of all twenty-nine men who went down with her. Carpenter had an uncle who had sailed to the bottom of Lake Superior on that great ship. The song brought him to tears.

Carpenter and Frenic could not believe their eyes when they reached their home port. The population of Saint Renee had nearly tripled. They literally sailed into port with their mouths open. Boats of all shapes and sizes crowded the channel. It was like five o'clock traffic in downtown Dallas.

The docks were as busy as they had been in two centuries. Sherry was in the middle of the madness directing traffic. She saw the Deliverance tie up in her slip and called for Carpenter and Frenic to join her.

"I had a large crate come in while you were gone. Would you two be sweet and move it to the entrance of the Marina," she asked as she batted her eyes at them.

"What does she do that for?" Carpenter asked her boyfriend in a joking manner. "She already knows we're going to do whatever she says anyway."

They all met up later that night at the Yellow Rose for a special dinner for Bubba's closest friends. Someone was missing and it struck Carpenter as a little odd. He asked to have a word with Sherry in the kitchen.

"Sherry, did you invite Captain Boulet?" he asked, noticing the missing member of the party.

"I did but never got a response, Sherry stated. "So I sent Jim Moore to see what was up. He came back with some sad news. He was told Boulet started losing his mind shortly after he returned from looking for Bubba. Someone went to check on him about a month ago and he was gone.

"No one has seen hide nor hair of him since. It's sad, real sad. I was going to tell you after this was over. One missing person at a time, you know?"

"Yes I see your point," said Carpenter. "But you said 'this.' Just what are you calling 'this?' I mean does it have a name?"

"Sure it does," Sherry said taking him by the hand to the back of the kitchen. "Don't tell nobody. I am having these banners put up tonight," she said as she unrolled one. The banner read 'Come ride with McBride'

"I like it, I like it a lot," Carpenter said.

The dinner had a mixture of people from all walks of life. In one corner of the room sat Carpenter with his and Bubba's army buddies. In another corner sat the who's who of Texas horse royalty: Rodeo's World Champion, Bronc Von Kurtz; the cutting world's Triple Crown winner, Bill Freeman; Trainer of the year Shawn Kelly and a few more, including Chubby Turner.

In another part of the room were Bubba's secret society brothers: Dr. Johnny Two Feathers and Billy and Dusty Johnson. Still in another part of the room were the sailors who had befriended him. Sherry made sure she left one seat open for Captain Boulet - just in case.

Sherry, Doc, Captain Frenic and Jim Moore sat at the main table. Also sitting with them was Sherry's and Bubba's cousin Lucius Defoe of the Texas

Rangers. Everyone in attendance made it an event to remember with toasting and Bubba Lee stories going way into the night.

Carpenter woke up the next morning with the undeniable scent of roasting beef. The smell was irresistible for any red-meat-eating American. He went to the Yellow Rose but the heavenly aroma wasn't coming from there. His nose led him to the village square where he could not believe his eyes.

"Sherry knows how to pull out all the stops," he said to himself.

He would never have believed in the middle of an island village, in the Caribbean Sea, he'd be looking at a nineteenth-century chuck wagon. It took him awhile just to take it all in. He walked toward the wagon as soon as he knew he wasn't dreaming or that he and his army buddies hadn't downed one too many the night before.

He was met with, "Good morning there, pard. I'd be Rodney, the wagon master. That ugly feller over there cutting up the spuds, that be Ben. And that pretty thing over yonder, that be Ben's wife Cassy. She's a looker but blind as a bat. She'd have to be to get hitched to ole Ben. You're our first visitor this morning. Could you do with a cup of coffee?"

Carpenter took the man up on his coffee. It was strong as hell and reminded him of the coffee his old man would brew when he was a kid ice fishing on the Great Lakes. Rodney wasn't acting the part of a cow poke; he was the ranch manager on the 3-C ranch. He and Bubba had run together as young men.

His morning at the chuck wagon would set the scene for all things to come that day. It was one surprise after another. Rodney and his crew put on one hell of a feed at noon, a meal that even The Big Tex in Amarillo would be jealous of.

Sherry told everyone to come down to the entrance of the Marina when they had finished eating. She said she had a surprise for everyone. Carpenter being Carpenter got a little curious and wandered down a little early. Sherry must have had a band of magical mystics or something because there was a stage that wasn't there the day before. In the center of the entrance was whatever Sherry had in the crate. It had to have been unpacked in the night and had a tarp over it. Carpenter was on his way to have a look under the tarp when Sherry caught him.

"Don't you think you ought to wait for everyone else?" she said, scolding him.

He felt like a child who nearly got his hand caught in the cookie jar. "Yes Ma'am! Sherry I pray if something ever happens to me, they put you in charge," he joked.

"Why, nobody would show up but bartenders, hookers, and ex's," she joked right back.

"Yes, but those are my people," he replied.

It didn't take long for the crowd's curiosity to get the best of them, just like Carpenter's. Within twenty minutes of her announcement, hundreds of people surrounded the stage.

"BUBBA, BUBBA, BUBBA," they chanted.

Sherry took the stage with microphone in hand. "Friends are we having fun yet! My brother Bubba, he loved life. He lived everyday like it was his last. Don't you think we ought to do the same?" she asked and the crowd cheered

"Bubba was a simple man who loved his family, his friends and he loved Jester. He loved this island because it gave him the one thing he never had: a childhood. He was a dreamer that wasn't afraid to dream and share his dreams with those he loved. Jon and I are living proof. I wanted to give you all a small reminder of my brother, Jester and you own dreams," she concluded giving a sign.

Some men pulled the tarp off the object in the entranceway. The crowd gasped and then began to cheer. Hiding under the tarp was a sculptured bust of Bubba Lee and Jester. The inscription read "Bubba Lee McBride and Jester, lost but not forgotten".

"You did good, real good," Carpenter told her when he joined her on stage.

"Now are you all ready to get down, the Texas way?" she asked before she introduced the first act.

The island party for the beloved Captain Cowboy went on until the wee hours of the morning. Everyone said goodbye in their own way. Everyone except Sherry; she would never tell her brother goodbye.

It was right before the dawn and Sherry was standing on the dock looking out to sea, the way she had for over a year. She heard Jon Carpenter's voice behind her.

"You were right. If Bubba finds out he missed this shindig, he's gonna be pissed," he said in a loving way.

The deserted island Bubba Lee had washed up on wasn't the same place a year later. He had added a lot of civic improvements in the time he had been there. The island had a new transit system thanks to the miles of trails he had carved out of the jungle. The farthest point on the island could be reached in no more than forty-five minutes, with the help of both his trail and zip-line systems.

He almost felt like Tarzan swinging though the trees each time he flew through them on his zip line. He even fashioned a harness out of canvas for Jester. He knew if he was found, he would be famous with a flying dog.

He had cultivated a plot by the stream he and Jester first drank from and put in a garden. The jungle was alive with lots of vegetation, fruits, berries and a few vegetables. Bubba reasoned, "Why spend his time searching for them when he could grow them all on the same plot?"

He had captured wild hogs and tried to domesticate and breed them. He had fresh meat year round but still he built a crude smoke house. He didn't have any eggs but at least he could have bacon for breakfast. Jester appreciated the meat because he could only take so much fruit.

The shelter he had built when they had first arrived had been turned into a storage unit. It took him three months but he had built him a thing of beauty: a one-bedroom, two-story, bamboo condominium that rose out of the island's floor.

His new digs came with a wood cook stove he had made from parts off the German U-boat. He had also devised his own water and septic system. The Romans of old didn't have damn thing on a Texan. The day he finished his master piece he marveled,

"You reckon that Robin Leach feller would do a show on us? He could call it Lifestyle of the Rich and Shipwrecked," he said, joking with his dog.

Bubba worked hard every day, sometimes sixteen hours a day. He chopped, hauled, pulled and sawed until his hands and back ached. He did it for several reasons but mainly he worked hard so he wouldn't go crazy.

The dead German soldiers he had found when he first landed on the island had left an impression on him. They had more than likely gone crazy and killed one another. It was the last thing he intended happening to him. It was better to have an ache in the back than a bullet in the head.

It didn't seem to matter how hard he worked, he had always felt like he was not alone, and sometimes he could feel eyes on him. It was a feeling he couldn't seem to shake.

He tried to explain the feeling away in the beginning, using a number of different reasons. The simple one was: it was his over-active imagination.

He would have liked to believe it was angels watching out for him. It could be the ghost of all those who had lost their lives on the island, who's to say.

Bubba laughed it off at first, and when that stopped working he tried to put it out of his head. It wasn't long before some strange things started to occur. He would go to work in the morning, come home, and food would be missing.

He thought it was Jester double dipping at first but then there were times when Jester was with him and it still happened. It could have been some island critter he thought, but then things started being rearranged. He'd leave his cup one side of his house and he'd come back and it would be on the other side. It was getting a little spooky.

Something kept Bubba awake one night. He tossed and turned and sleep could not be had. Something was nagging at him but he didn't know what. A walk on the beach seemed like a good course of action. He tried to get Jester to go with him, but the dog wouldn't bulge.

"Suit yourself, you lazy-ass mutt," he muttered and off he went.

Sun rise was still a couple hours away but the full moon lit the path to the beach. It took him back to his last night in Saint. Renee; that point in time seemed more like a hundred years ago, yet it was only one.

Perhaps it was thoughts of his sister that drove him from his rack. He wished there was a way he could let her know he was alive and well. He could only guess how much she was suffering. He hoped Captain Frenic still had her heart; she deserved to be happy.

It was true that he missed her but he wasn't sure that was why he couldn't sleep. A day hadn't gone by that he hadn't missed her; it was already baked in the pie, so to speak. It had to be something if it wasn't her.

Perhaps it was those pestering ghosts again; they were on Bubba's nerves. It wasn't bad enough that he felt he was being watched during the day, the spooks had started invading his sleep.

He was beginning to think it wasn't his thoughts of Saint Renee, Sherry, or the ghost keeping awake; more than likely it was his own silly imagination. It took him over an hour and a mile of beach to reach that conclusion.

The sun was on its way up and he was about to turn around and head for home. All of a sudden he saw tracks and they weren't animal tracks. It felt like he was dreaming and perhaps he wasn't having trouble sleeping after all.

He bent down to examine the foot prints. They were too small to belong to a man. He was certain they either belonged to a woman or a half-grown child. The question was not who they belonged to but how they got there. Why would a woman or child be on the island and why hadn't he known?

Those were just a few of the many questions he had as he decided to follow the tracks. He had two main questions: "Was there a way off the island?" and "Were there any other people on the island?" He also wondered if this was what had been keeping him awake at night.

Bubba followed the footprints down the shoreline for another hundred yards. Then they turned and went inland. He followed them onward through the jungle until he came to a clearing he didn't remember seeing before.

He came to a stop in the brush when he saw the person he was tracking asleep by a fire. Bubba couldn't tell who the person was because they had their back toward him. His first thought was to go and wake them but he chose not to act rash. He'd just hunker down and wait; after all, hadn't they been watching him sleep? No good could come out of a surprise attack and if it was a child or woman; he would just frighten them.

It wasn't long before he heard someone or something else coming through the jungle toward the clearing. Bubba sank down in the brush deeper. He couldn't help but to think it might be another person.

His heart began to beat faster and faster as the sounds came closer. He had a lump in his throat until he saw Jester come be-bopping out of the jungle. The dog strolled into the clearing like he'd been there a hundred times.

Bubba tried to get his dog's attention before a train wreck occurred before his eyes. He could only imagine someone waking to find the massive dog hovering over them. It would be enough to give anyone a heart attack. If that happened, he'd be the only one on the island again.

Jester did not see nor hear his master. He walked right to the sleeping body and licked it in the face, just like he often did to his owner. The person rose up and for the first time Bubba saw it was a beautiful young woman. Much to his surprise she reached out and began to stroke the dog.

"Some watch dog you are. Jester, you've been holding out on me," Bubba Lee said under his breath.

He slowly stood as so she could see his presence. He figured, "Why should he be the only one shocked that morning?" He moved carefully so as to not frighten the woman. "I think he likes you," he spoke in a soft voice.

The woman was startled and she jumped up to face him. It was then Bubba caught sight of just how beautiful the woman was. His heart began to race again but for a totally different reason.

The woman began to back away at the sight of Bubba. "I won't hurt you, miss. I just want to be friends," he spoke in a calm voice.

Bubba bent down and called Jester to him. The dog did as he was directed. He began to pet Jester as a way to prove to her he meant her no harm. "See I won't hurt you," he said turning his attention back to the woman.

He then realized he would have to earn her trust and it wasn't happening then. He looked into her beautiful dark eyes, "I won't intrude any longer Ma'am. I hope in time you and I can become friends," he said to the only human being he had seen in over a year.

"Jester you can stay with your friend, I'll see you back at camp. And son, you got some explaining to do," Bubba said as he turned to walk away.

He had so many different thoughts as he made his way back. How did such a beautiful creature come to be on the island? He was pretty sure she was alone, so who left her there? How long had she been there? These were the questions he would ponder on his way back to his place on the island.

It was his sister Sherry who preyed on his mind just hours earlier. But a different woman captured his every thought as he worked through the day. He couldn't put his finger on it, but there was something about her that made an impression on him. Maybe it was the mere fact he had been alone too long.

It was enough that he was driving himself crazy with his thoughts of her, but he started wondering what she was thinking. But he realized that's one thing no man should ever do. He felt she must have some thoughts. Who knows how long she'd been watching him. She didn't run, so he took that much as a good sign.

He knew one thing for sure as the day came to an end: the island would never be the same.

It was late in the afternoon when Jester returned. "Well did you have a good time, boy?" Bubba said to his dog. "What I wouldn't give at this moment if you could talk. I'd give twice as much to trade places with you," he told the secret-keeping mutt.

Supper came and went, as Bubba watched the 390th day on the island come to a close. The day had been one of surprises, for sure. He thought of one of Doc's earlier stories about a princess and he wondered if he hadn't seen one in person that day. He would be her friend he told himself before drifting off to sleep.

PARADISE FOUND

Chapter 8

The courtship between the hardened, one-time cowboy and his island princess went slowly and awkwardly. Bubba started leaving fish in her clearing whenever he and Jester went fishing. On one occasion, he left a blanket right before a storm. He looked for any reason to pass by the clearing, hoping to see the young woman. Sometimes he would catch sight of her and sometimes she would smile.

The few smiles made his hopes dive deeper inside his heart. He was visiting places he hadn't been in a very long time. He was falling in love with a woman who had never said a single word to him.

One day he was gathering fruit along the cliffs that overlooked the ocean. He just happened to look up at the time she dove into the water. Her dark brown, naked body overwhelmed him to the point where he forgot all about the fruit. He didn't gaze at her with lustful eyes; his eyes held only to the beauty of her form.

It was a day unlike any other he had spent on the island. He had been on the other side of the island working. He returned to his lodge, tired from his day, only find his supper had already been prepared. Jester had been with him so he knew it wasn't the dog's doings. There was only one other possibility and that possibility warmed his heart.

She was nowhere in sight but her actions proved Bubba was making progress. He tasted the food and he smiled. "I wonder what her chicken-fried steak tastes like?" he thought in a humorous manner.

It had been some time since a woman had fussed over him. Great food, a touched heart, and a feeling he was finally connecting with. In his eyes it didn't get any better than that. But it did as soon as the thought formed.

The biggest surprise of all he caught from corner of his eye. He saw her standing in the evening's shadows. Bubba rose to his feet as a sign of respect. Without thinking, he motioned for her to join him. She just smiled before giving in to his invitation.

Bubba reached inside the door of his hut and pulled out a chair he had made for her. He set it by the fire for her and then backed away. He had worked too hard for that one moment and didn't want to crowd her. She was even more beautiful close up in the fire's light.

"My name is Bubba," he said as he took his seat.

She smiled but he could tell she hadn't a clue what he had said.

"I'm Bubba," He said pointing at himself.

"The second time worked like a charm. "Bu,,,,bba" she stammered. "Nasus," she said pointing at herself.

He heard the name and repeated it out loud. It wasn't near as pretty as when she said it and yet it might have been the prettiest he had ever heard. She smiled as he said it a second time. The weeks of not knowing her name were over, as was the admiring her from afar.

Not much was shared between the two over their first meal. A smile here and a smile there but it was all he had hoped it would be. It didn't seem to matter that they spoke different tongues; their body language said volumes.

Time passed and before he knew it their evening was almost as an end. Nasus motioned it was time for her to go. He wanted more than anything to walk her back to her clearing but he didn't know how. Something in him told her what his words couldn't. She went to him and took his hand and motioned for him to come with her. It was something he did gladly.

The night was filled with the music of the jungle. They walked hand in hand along the beach, the very same stretch of beach where he had first seen her tracks in the sand. The moon even seemed to be in cahoots with the moment by shining down and lighting their way.

Bubba's head filled with words he wanted to say but he knew she would not understand one of them. It had been years since he had those feelings and he could not even tell her. It would be easy for him to get frustrated but he didn't, because he saw the brighter side. He wasn't going anywhere, she wasn't going anywhere and they had nothing but time. The only hope he had was that she felt the same way.

They were standing in her clearing before they knew it. She sat on a rock while he built her a fire. It seemed to be the least he could do after the fire she had started in him. The time had come to say goodnight even though it was the last thing he wanted to do. He told Jester to stay behind to keep her company and just like that he was gone.

The next morning he awoke to the scent of breakfast being cooked. He looked outside to see Nasus hovering over a morning fire. Her hair shone as her matching eyes sparkled in the morning's light. He was amazed. Never in all his years had he seen such raw beauty. It was nothing short of a man in love.

He smiled as he remembered the old story about being on a deserted island with a beautiful woman. It was every man's dream and his reality.

The two were together every waking hour from that point on. They learned to communicate first in sign language. She learned some of his words and he learned some of hers; together they formed their own language.

Together they built another room on to his grass estate. He told her it was for her only after it was finished. He watch as a grown woman turned into a little girl before his eyes. She jumped for joy and then jumped into his arms. Bubba Lee held the beautiful Nasus in his arms for the first time.

He was lost to the world and yet he was found for the first time in his life. He felt the grace he had always longed for every time he looked into her eyes. It was then he realized what Sherry had tried to tell him that night so long ago.

The feelings everyone needs cannot be met by just anyone, not even him. Nasus could give him what Sherry never could, just as Captain Tony could give her what Bubba never could. Days drifted by and he found himself falling deeper and deeper in love with her.

One day it occurred to him that he had never asked how she came to be on the island. He was so caught up with his feelings toward her, it had slipped his mind. She was telling him how funny he looked his first day, trying to pull all his rafts off the reef. He wasn't even aware he was being watched.

He asked Nasus how she got to the island when their laughter had ended. He saw a sad look overtake the normally happy woman. She relived the day, fifteen years earlier, almost in tears. Bubba was sorry he even brought the subject up.

Nasus's family had set out one morning to a neighboring island. It was the time of year when the small islands came together for trade. They had been out to sea a number of hours when a storm blew up. The small craft her family was in capsized. She had watched her family drown, one by one as she clung to the side of the boat. She was adrift for days until, like him, she was saved by the island. She had come to the island as a teenager and had grown to be woman. She was crying when the tale came to an end.

Bubba put his arms around her for comfort. "Bubba not leave Nasus, Bubba not leave Nasus," she repeated.

"No Ma'am, Bubba is yours always," he said knowing it to be the truest thing he had ever said.

"Nasus loves Bubba Lee," she said before their first kiss. Her lips were like a breath of life to a dying man, each kiss sweeter than the last. Her body melted into his, and his into hers. He knew she was his for the taking.

He wanted her so badly that it ached to refuse himself such pleasure. He wanted something more, more than just the illusion of love; more than the passion of the moment. He wanted it all and he wanted it forever. The tide came in and chased the lovers from the beach but nothing would chase her from his mind.

A year and a half had come and gone since Bubba had the little run in with the hurricane. The first year was spent trying to keep his hopes up of ever getting off the island. He was beginning to think that was not a possibility. He hadn't even seen the hint of a boat or a plane.

The reality was he might never see Sherry, Jon Carpenter or anyone from his former life. The aspect might have been unbearable before but with Nasus, it was just another problem that had turned into a delightful opportunity.

The long and short of it was, he was going to ask his beautiful island princess to be his wife. The only problem with that was how. It wasn't like they could hop the next flight to Vegas and find a wedding chapel complete with a look-alike Elvis.

It dawned on him that one of the laws of the sea was a Captain could perform weddings. He was a little fuzzy on rather or not a Captain could perform his own wedding but that seemed beside the point. He might be on the island for the rest of his life, but with Nasus as his wife, it seemed like a pretty good life.

Coming up with the how's proved to be the easy part. Explaining to her what it all meant was the real chore. She would have said yes to any request he made, so it was important to him that she understood the question before he asked it.

He asked her if she remembered what her father was to her mother, and what her mother was to her father. She looked at him funny and told him that she did. He then told her it was what he wished for them.

It took a few minutes for her to figure out what the clumsy cowboy was trying to ask. Her eyes lit up with joy when she realized the question. "Yes I love Bubba, I Love Bubba," she said throwing her arms around his neck and kissing him.

He saw for one brief moment the reaction to that one particular question was universal. Her joy would be the same in any culture. His reaction to hers almost brought him to tears as the two of them soaked in the memory of that moment in time.

The next morning Bubba got handed another surprise, in the way of his breakfast and his bedroll.

"Bubba go now. Nasus get ready. Bubba meet Nasus two days on beach. Bubba go, take Jester too," she told him.

"Come on boy. So much of a home being a man's castle," he said jokingly, knowing full well that he might have been the Captain, but he'd never again be boss.

It was like his old buddy Shawn Kelly once told him. "When you say 'I do,' it's the last free choice you'll ever make. From then on son, it's 'Yes Ma'am, you're right baby and no honey your butt's not that big.' Get used to it 'cause it won't change." Bubba laughed at the old memory.

Bubba had gone through the marriage deal before but had forgotten how nervous a man could get. He paced back and forth on the other side of the island for two days. It wasn't at all like his last wedding; the boys were not around to throw him a stag party.

He got so drunk at his that he forgot how nervous he truly was.

"What do you say Jester, you gonna get a few strippers and show me what I'll be missing," he asked his one constant companion.

The day came when Bubba stood on the beach waiting for his new bride. His joy did what the whiskey had done years before: taken away his nerves. He hadn't gotten much sleep the night before and he hoped he wouldn't be getting much that night.

He saw her coming toward him from a quarter mile away. His heart skipped a beat much like the first time he saw her. She never looked so beautiful and in his eyes no women ever could. He noticed everything about her: from the flowers in her hair to the dress made from one of his pearl-snap shirts. He marveled how much better it looked on her.

The closer she came, the more he noticed the glow that surrounded her. It told him her feelings for him ran just as deep as his for her. He couldn't help it. He found himself walking toward her, then taking her hand and kissing her. He knew he was lost to the world but he was enjoying every minute of it.

He began to speak the words he had memorized, and when he finished she repeated them back to him in her own tongue. God witnessed a thing of beauty that day and blessed two of his children.

The whole thing didn't take more than ten minutes and then he picked her up in his arms and carried back to their home with Jester right behind them. It was alright until they got back and the dog tried to follow them inside. "I think I got this boy," Bubba said with a smile as he shut the door.

Another year passed Bubba by like it was nothing. He had settled into a normal, married life or as normal as life could be between two people and a dog stranded on an island. He had long since given up on being rescued and did not know how one was rescued from paradise. The only regret he had was the loss Sherry must have been feeling. He hoped in his heart of hearts she had found happiness.

Jester, like his master, was growing fat and sassy. Nasus kept the boys well fed and loved. Bubba would go to bed each night thinking he couldn't love her any more, only to wake and find he had been wrong the night before.

The two did everything together and shared every thought. It was the reason he became concerned one morning when he woke up alone. He scanned the house, no Nasus. He went outside, again she was nowhere in sight. He called and heard no answer. Jester seemed to be missing as well.

Bubba was halfway to the beach when he heard her faint cries. He ran as fast as he could in the direction of the sound. Nasus was doubled over on her hands and knees when he found her. She was heaving up what little was left in her stomach.

"What's the matter sweetheart? Did you eat something bad last night," he asked holding her head.

She was frightened and talking as fast as she could in her native tongue. He had no idea what she was saying. It dawned on him that it might be possible she had never been sick before, or perhaps when she was a child, and didn't remember it.

"It's alright Nasus, everyone gets sick every now and then. It was just something you ate more than likely," he told her in a comforting voice.

He waited until she was ready then he helped her to her feet. She was back to her normal self by the time they reached home. It puzzled him briefly but she looked no worse for wear. Bubba still checked in on her throughout the day, and at the end of the day, it was like it never happened.

The next morning he was awakened by the same sounds he had heard the day before. She wasn't able to make it to the jungle was the only difference. The day played out about the same and she was fine in a few hours. The third day began the same way but by then Bubba had figured it out, or the best a cowboy could.

He didn't know how he was going to tell her what they had been doing nearly every morning had caused the sickness. He had no idea how she was going to react when he told her she was with child either. He was so happy he was beside himself and hoped she would be as well.

Bubba sat her down after the third bout of morning sickness had run its course. "Nasus, we are going to have a baby," he blurted out, not being able to control his joy.

She looked at her husband like he had lost his mind. He saw her disbelief and began to tell her that her morning sickness was brought on by being pregnant.

Her question was, "What caused the pregnancy that had caused the morning sickness?" Bubba found himself having a conversation he never dreamed that he would be having with his wife; maybe a son years later.

A son - that sounded so good. Or a daughter! He was caught up in the moment. His joy became her joy as soon as Nasus was sure her Bubba wasn't crazy.

Nasus became larger as the months went by. Bubba assured her every step of the way that her body was behaving normal. He told her she would return to her normal size after the baby came. He was amazed with himself, what the hell did he know about pregnant women. He faked almost everything just so she wouldn't worry.

It was one thing to reassure his trusting wife and another thing to assure himself. He knew he would have to deliver their child and it scared the hell out of him. He had pulled calves and helped with the birth of many a colt. But a child of his own..... He would later tell himself that was the moment he became a praying man.

Bubba knew with the help of the good Lord he might be able to pull off the impossible. He had been doing the impossible longer than he could remember. The hurricane alone should have killed him. He knew in his heart the impossible was made possible only by the Master.

It was true so much had been taken throughout his life but in turn, so much had been given. It was hard to deny the Lord hadn't been with him his entire life. He just prayed He would be with him when the baby came.

He knew the Lord would be there when the time came, there was no doubt about that. He just wished the time would get there. He might have known where babies came from, but he had no idea where his pregnant wife's mood swings were coming from. She would be beautifully glowing one minute and in tears the next.

To keep his mind from driving himself sick with worry, he began a little project, one he had hope would bring a smile to his wife's face. Every morning he would go out and work on it alone. He left Jester to keep watch and keep Nasus company.

She was nearing the end of her term by the time Bubba had his surprise finished. He was unaware she had been keeping up with the hours he spent away from her or what her moods were telling her.

He heard her crying before he reached the door. He sat his gift in the bushes and then went to comfort her. "Why is my Nasus crying?" he asked as he entered their home.

"Bubba don't love Nasus. Nasus fat and ugly, Bubba stay gone all day," she cried.

"Bubba does love Nasus, Bubba may go crazy unless this baby hurries, but Bubba will always love you," he swore. He held her in his arms until she stopped crying. As he did, he hummed a soft tune to her.

"I got something for Nasus," he told her after she had calmed down. He took her by the hand and led her outside. "Nasus, sit here and Bubba will show you what he's been up to," he instructed.

She was almost child-like by that point, doing as she was asked. He waited until she was settled then went to the bushes where he had hid her surprise. "See my princess, this is why I have been gone so much," he said as he pulled a bamboo cradle from the underbrush. "This is for you and the baby," he told her.

Nasus's tears vanished as she clapped her hands. A smile gripped her face and she motioned for her husband to bring the cradle closer. She kissed him and began to cry again.

"Now why does Nasus cry," he wanted to know.

"Bubba loves Nasus," she explained. "Nasus cries when she thinks Bubba don't love her.

Nasus cries when Bubba loves her, said Bubba. "Girl, that baby can't get here soon enough to suit me," he said, once again taking her into his arms.

Nasus's time was getting close. Each day that passed meant they were closer to seeing their child. Bubba or Jester always seemed to be by her side. The last few weeks of her pregnancy she found it difficult to get around. Her overprotective husband didn't let her stray too far from the bed.

One day he heard her scream while he was cleaning fish. He dropped everything and ran to her as fast as he could. Bubba found her standing up and holding her belly. Her body was soaked with sweat and her fists were clinched as a bolt of pain ran through her. He knew it was her time and the puddle of water beneath her told him she was already in labor.

He laid her on her back and began to try to calm her down. He had been doing his best to prepare her for weeks. It was not an easy task, he being a man and her never seeing a baby being born. Another shot of pain went through Nasus about the time he got her calm.

"Everything is going to be alright; just listen to my voice," Bubba said as he made his way to the foot of the bed. "Do you trust me, Nasus?" he asked as he raised her dress and spread her legs. She shook her head, 'yes.' "

"Remember we talked about this; you know what to do. Push when I tell you to, like now, push." The pitch of his voiced never changed as he talked her through the delivery.

"Push now, I can see the head. Alright girl, one more to get the shoulders out and we are done," and with those last words a new McBride came into the world.

"Hello Missy, welcome home," Bubba Lee proudly said to his daughter who was resting in his arms for the first time. She was red and wrinkled and yet the most beautiful sight his eyes had ever gazed upon.

Nasus rested while Bubba cut the cord and cleaned the baby girl up. He could tell she was dark skinned like her mother but she had blonde hair. The color of the baby's hair reminded him of his little sister, Sherry. He wondered what she might think if she could see him holding his new daughter.

"You would love your aunt Sherry, I know you would," he said to the baby.

He didn't know his wife was listening to him. "Bubba bring her to me, bring Nasus Little Sherry. I want to see," she said when she gave her newborn her name. He was pleased with the name and carefully carried the child to her waiting mother but the baby began to cry.

"Bubba, Little Sherry not like me," Nasus said with tears in her eyes.

"No Nasus, Little Sherry hungry," Bubba laughed as he showed her how to breast feed.

He then turned for the door. "Where Bubba go," she asked.

"To tell Jester, then I might go howl at the moon," Bubba said walking on air. "Jester we got us a little girl. Can you believe that, I finally got it right. She's a pretty thing. I wish I could tell the world,' Bubba told his best friend. He stood up, "I am a daddy" he yelled as loud as he could.

The days that followed brought a shining light in the old cowboy's eyes. The light could be summed up in one word: fatherhood. The McBrides were a real family, mother, father, child and dog. It couldn't have been any more normal on any street in America.

Days grew into weeks and weeks grew into months. The next thing Bubba knew, his daughter was two years old. Some four and half years were between the old cowboy and a small village named Saint Renee.

He saw both the women he loved in his daughter's eyes. Her hair was long and looked like spun gold. Every now and then when he looked at her, he saw his little sister looking back.

Little Sherry would reach out and grab his heart sometimes, just like her mother. Her temper, and, yes she had one that he figured she got from her mother and her aunt. Since he was the only man, he wore the brunt of more than one dissatisfaction.

Bubba would tell her stories at night until she fell asleep. He would then sit there and watch her sleep until Nasus came for him. "Bubba, she'll be there in the morning, come to bed," said Nasus, whose English by now was nearly perfect.

Bubba would no sooner leave and Jester would take his place. Not only did he lose his heart to the child, but he lost his dog as well. Everywhere Little Sherry wandered, Jester was not far behind. He would lie on the beach and let the little girl bury him in sand. Jester would stand and shake and they would do it all over again.

One more year flew by before Bubba would once again feel pain. Pain like he had never felt.

Nasus fell ill during the rainy season. First they thought it was just a cold; she always seemed to get them around monsoons. A cold then turned into a fever she could not shake. It wasn't long before she couldn't get out of bed.

Day and night Bubba sat by her side praying; praying to the same God who saved him from the storm, the same God who had blessed their love with a child. He wiped her forehead with a cool rag when the fever became unbearable. He held her shaking body next to his when the chills came.

He did all he knew to do and still he never felt so helpless. He had never loved anyone as much as he loved Nasus. He knew he was losing her and it was tearing him to pieces. He began to curse the island he had loved for so long. He knew if there was only a doctor, she would be fine.

Bubba had fallen asleep in the early morning hours after sitting up two days straight with Nasus. He was awakened by her faint voice calling his name. He opened his eyes and reached for her hand. "I am here my princess, I just drifted off for a moment," he confessed.

"Bubba, it's hard to say goodbye to someone you love. It hurts me so to leave you and Little Sherry. I have been watching you sleep and trying to find the right words to say. I love you and our daughter so much. That's all I can think of.

"I can see in my husband's eyes, this is hurting him, but you have to be strong for Little Sherry. You have to find a way off this island and take her with you. You have to go back to your people, back to those who love you and will love our little girl. Don't let her grow up alone on this island like me. She'll never find the love I had. Go home Bubba, it's time.

"Think of me when you see our daughter's smile. Remember me when you hear her laugh. These are the ways I will live, these are the ways you will always know I love you." She closed her eyes for the last time after finished speaking.

The once hardened cowboy collapsed with pain. His body fell on hers as a river of tears flowed from the eyes of a man some wondered would ever cry.

"Please don't go, please. God please don't take my Nasus. Take me, take me, but let her live," he pleaded over and over.

He picked her up in his arms and held her limp body close to him. All the love and the memories they had shared went through his mind. "I will love you forever, my Nasus, my island princess," Bubba said through his tears. The sun met the day as heartbreak rained down on the man.

The sweetest voice broke through the silence, broke through the sorrow of his heart and numbed him from the pain. It was the voice of his daughter. "Momma, daddy, are you awake?" the sounds of his little girl brought him back from his grief and to Nasus's final words, "Be strong for our daughter," would ring in his ears for days to come."

Quickly he gathered himself, and then placed a blanket over his wife's body. He had to kiss her one last time before covering her face. He then moved toward the sound of his daughter's voice. He turned one more time, he couldn't help but think part of him died in that room moments earlier.

The first thing he saw when he entered her room was Little Sherry playing with Jester on the floor. He might have wanted to join Nasus but the sight proved he had so much to live for.

The little girl looked up when she heard her daddy enter the room. "Daddy, is momma feeling better?" the child asked. The question alone burned a hole right through his heart. The tears started to swell up in his eyes, but he fought them back.

He picked her from off the floor and held her tight. Bubba carried his daughter out the door and down the path to the beach. He called to Jester and the dog ran after him. He took her to the place she always played at and sat her in the sand. Her bucket was there from the night before.

The little girl had no way of knowing what had transpired earlier and began to play, just as though it was any other day. Bubba looked hopelessly out to sea, wanting to find the words to tell Little Sherry her mother was gone. Bubba knew deep down the words could not be found in the surf. The words would have to come from his heart, but his heart was shattered.

Slowly the words fell from his lips, "Last night while you lay sleeping, the angels came. Your momma was so sick and hurt so bad that they thought it best for her to go with them. They took her to a place called heaven, where there is no sickness or pain. Your momma didn't want to go because she loved you so much but her pain was so bad that she had no choice.

"She told me to tell you not to cry, because she loves you. She also said to tell you she would always live in your heart and you would never be alone. She'll be with you every time you think of her," he concluded.

He was in tears when he finished. Little Sherry hugged his neck, "Remember daddy, momma said not to cry," she reminded him.

"I'll try sweetheart, I'll try," was about all he could say.

Bubba Lee stayed with his daughter a while longer to make sure she was alright. It was a blessing that she was too young to realize fully what was happening.

"Why don't you stay here and play with Jester," he told his little girl. "Daddy has some things to do at home."

"Jester, you stay here with little Sherry; you take care of my little girl for me, I'll be back shortly," he said to the dog.

Bubba thought about his old dog on his way back to the house. He thought how much he had relied on him throughout the years. He knew he would have never made it this far without him; he had trusted everything to him. He knew as long as Jester was around, his daughter would be safe.

He didn't know which was harder: telling his daughter that her mother was gone or moving his beloved wife's body from the house until he could say his final goodbyes after Little Sherry went to bed that night.

Gently he uncovered her to prepare her for burial later on that night. He was frightened at first over what he found and then warmed. Nasus had left him with one last smile, a smile that would carry him though the rest of his life.

He gently washed her pale body before dressing her in the dress she had made when they took their vows. He brushed her long black hair one last time before wrapping her tightly in a thick blanket. Bubba carried her gently outside. A thousand feet away, there was a rock ledge. It is where he placed Nasus's body until their last walk together.

He made sure her precious body was secured before he returned to the beach. Bubba went back to the house and grabbed some fruit for Little Sherry because he knew she would be hungry. He figured they would spend the day there and he would let her play herself out.

The last place he wanted to be was in a house that no longer contained his wife's voice. So Bubba sat on the beach all day with his pain and with his daughter. She would look back at him and he would remember something else he was going to miss about her mother. He learned that the first day without his soul mate would not be easy.

Toward the end of the day, Little Sherry told him she was getting hungry. He gathered her up and took her back home where he fixed her a bite to eat. The little girl climbed up in her daddy's lap when she was finished and said, "Daddy, tell me a story," just like she requested every night.

He knew as sure as the sun came up, Little Sherry would want her story time. He didn't know if he would have been able to tell her a story if she would've asked earlier. He was ready for a story by the time she asked.

"Once upon a time there was this crazy old cowboy who rode a wild hurricane all the way to the island. He was lost and alone, except for his faithful dog.

All he had loved was way far, far away. He was heartbroken until a beautiful island princess saved him." He went on and on, telling her the story of a lifetime.

Little Sherry was fast asleep by the time her father finished the story. He picked her up and took her to bed. Her daddy wouldn't be there to watch her sleep that night. Her day was over but his was a long way from conclusion.

Bubba Lee told Jester to watch after his daughter once again, just like he had done earlier. The time had come for him to take the last walk with his wife. He didn't know how he was going to manage it but it would be done by morning.

He slowly walked to where he had left Nasus's remains. The man grieved a little more with each step he took. His tears began to fall by the time he reached the ledge where he had left her earlier. He picked up what he would forever call his greatest treasure and began her funeral march.

The jungle was unusually silent that night. It was as if all who called the island home had felt the loss. Bubba Lee wandered aimlessly, first down one trail then another. His heart ached so much, he wasn't paying any attention Tears streamed down his face as he walked through the darkness.

Suddenly he found himself standing in the clearing where he had first seen the island princess. Was it fate, God, that her own spirit had led him to the clearing? He didn't know, nor did he question it. It was the perfect place to say goodbye, where a younger Bubba Lee had once said hello to a beautiful Nasus.

He prayed a lonely prayer once he had laid her in her final resting place. He didn't pretend to know the ways of the Creator and he didn't question them. He was angry that one more person was taken from him but who was he to question the ways of the Lord.

"I guess you needed her more than I did, Bubba said as he walked away. If you were looking for a new angel, Lord, you could not have found a better one."

WHEN THE COAST IS CLEAR

Chapter 9

Nasus's final words stuck with her husband for weeks, "Go home Bubba Lee, it's time." Bubba knew she was right; life would never be the same on the island without her. The question was just how to "go home." He hadn't even thought about the prospect in years. His love had given him a challenge and it was up to him to see it though.

Bubba pondered the question for days, with two options. He could do his best to build a boat and gather enough food for a voyage. He knew that option was a none-starter from the beginning. He and Jester had been on a boat with food before and that was how they landed on the island. He might have risked it anyway if not for his daughter. There was no way in hell he would take her off a safe island and put her adrift.

The old plan he had abandoned years earlier was all there was left. He had to start building signal fires again, that was the only way he could think of. He told himself he would go big, bigger than he ever dreamed, He'd build the son-of-a-bitch so big they'd be able to see the fire from The Cotton Bowl if he had to.

The idea took root and before long he was throwing himself into his work. He'd cut brush and drag it to the beach, then he'd cut trees and pull them to the sand. His fires would sometimes be twenty or thirty feet tall. The times when he would set one ablaze, the flames would climb a hundred feet in the air.

Bubba would be dead tired from the day's work, but he'd still be found in his chair watching his daughter sleep after their story time. Sometimes he'd half expected Nasus to come in Little Sherry's room and tell him to come to bed. But the love of his life, no matter how much he wanted it, never came.

It was true he worked hard at his task but he always made time to play with his daughter. She only had one parent left and Bubba made sure she wouldn't lose that one to his work. He also made sure they went to see Nasus's grave every chance they could. It was important to keep her memory alive, for both father and daughter.

One day on the beach, Bubba was building one of his signal fires while Little Sherry built castles in the sand. Jester lay calmly by the little girl as he always had. Bubba looked up from his work to find

239

the sky was growing darker. It wasn't just a summer squall; he had learned to tell the difference.

He could see flashes of lightning in the distance. Something told him it was what he and Nasus had termed a "caver." Bubba had long since cleaned out the cave he and Jester had found their first days on the island when he had buried the remains of the German soldiers. He and his family had ridden out more than one storm in the old cave. At one time, he and Nasus had spent a month fixing up the cave.

"I hate to cut this short guys but it's about for us to find the high ground," he told the dog and his little girl.

The storm had reached gale force by the time they made it to safety. All three of the McBride party were soaking wet. The cave was stocked with everything they might need including blankets. Bubba had gotten good over the years at salvaging usable items from the wrecks that dotted the island.

He wrapped Little Sherry in a blanket and then built a fire. His day of work had come to a sudden end so he thought he might as well take advantage of it.

"I'll fix us a bite to eat then I'll tell you a good, old-time, story," he promised.

Outside the storm raged on while Bubba spun his yarn of days of old in the Kingdom of Texas. The story was just King Author set on its head. In Bubba's tale, the Knights were cowboys with ropes who served King Stalbach. The dragons were replaced by giant armadillos and the evil kingdom was a place called Oklahoma.

Little Sherry had fallen asleep long before the story had ended, but that was her trend. Bubba thought she'd be a teenager before she ever heard the end of one of his stories and she would have probably grown out of story time by then.

He tucked her in the same way he had since the day she was born. He then went to the mouth of the cave to see what the storm was doing. He figured it might have died out by then, but if anything it was getting worse.

Bubba couldn't help but to think of the storm that he had fought years before. He had thought he had lost the battle, but looking at his sleeping little girl he knew he was the biggest winner of all. He returned to his post beside his daughter and marveled at how far he and his old mutt had come.

By daylight, it was like the storm had never happened. The sun was shining and the birds were singing; all seemed peaceful once again.. Bubba found Jester guarding the entrance when he woke up, "Just like a knight of old," he thought to himself.

He gathered up his daughter as soon as she had got awake. "Well baby girl, let's go see how bad it was," he told her once she was in his arms.

"Can we ride the Zipper today?" she asked referring to Bubba's zip line.

"Not today Sweetie, daddy needs to make sure it's safe," he explained.

Bubba would soon find out that nothing was as they had left it. The house he had built years before lay scattered from one side of the island to the other. His hog pens were destroyed but, thankfully, the wild pigs had scurried back into the jungle. Everything they owned that wasn't in the cave was flung haphazardly about them.

"Well Little Sherry, it's back to square one," he said looking at the mess, "but not today. Today we go fishing just as soon as your old man finds his poles and tackle box," he said smiling at the little girl.

Bubba was doing his best to tie a fly on the end of his line when he heard Little Sherry ask, "Daddy what's that?"

"What's what, honey?" Bubba asked, looking up to see a ship about a mile off shore. "It's a ship, by thunder, it's a ship," he yelled.

He ran as fast he could to his nearest signal fire. He did his best to set it ablaze but the storm had soaked the brush. He then remembered that his flare gun was in his tackle box.

Little Sherry must have thought he was playing a game as he raced back for his flare gun. Bubba put one flare in the chamber and prayed the thing still worked. The trigger was pulled and the flare shot out in the direction of the pile of brush. The flare ignited the wood just as he had hoped. He popped another flare in the gun and shot it into the air.

The first officer of a Caribbean freighter was busy scanning the horizon with a pair of field glasses. He spotted a flare racing through the air and followed it back to its origin. On the beach of the small island he saw a signal fire and then a man with a small child.

"Captain we have a situation on the bridge," the officer radioed below. He then brought the helm about and waited for his commanding officer.

"Look at this sir, it seems we have a distress signal," the mate said handing him the binoculars.

"I'll be damned, I don't believe this, I'll be damned," the Captain exclaimed.

"What is it sir?" his first mate wanted to know.

The stunned Captain paused before answering the question. "It's my long lost brother-in-law. Son, you just scored me a ton of points with the wife," he joked.

"You mean the cowboy? I thought he was dead," the puzzled man said.

"Everybody did, everybody but his sister. She never gave up on him," the Captain said.

"Drop the dingy, prepare to go ashore," the first mate ordered.

Soon the small boat was lowered and the crew awaited further orders. "You are in command Mr. Rogers. I'll be going ashore with the crew.

Bubba was just as surprised to see Captain Frenic coming to shore in the small craft. Little Sherry didn't know what to think she had never seen any people besides her parents. Jester ran up and down the shoreline sensing the excitement in the air.

Bubba picked up his little girl and went to greet the dingy. It seemed almost apropos it would be Frenic who found the lost cowboy since it was the argument over him that made Bubba a castaway.

"Tell me that's really you Tony," Bubba said as soon as he was in hearing distance.

"I could say the same thing. Hell there's no one any more shocked than I am right now," Captain Frenic answered back.

Both men were standing in the water, face to face by that time. Frenic noticed the small child in Bubba's arms. "Who's that you got there?" Frenic asked with a puzzled look.

"This is my daughter, Little Sherry," Bubba answered. He could see his answer had left the man even more dazed. Bubba handed the little girl to the Captain "It's a long story, Tony. Why don't we get out of the water and I'll tell it to you."

Gently the man took the child from her father, saying, "Come to your Uncle Tony."

Bubba saw the gold band around Frenic's finger after he said the word 'uncle.'

"Seems to me Tony, I ain't the only one with a story to tell," Bubba said, pointing at the ring.

Jester came running about that time. "I see you still have that old dog," Frenic said.

245

"To tell you the truth, I ain't sure who's got who," Bubba joked. "He might be better off if he'd stop following me around. Lord knows his love life would improve."

The topic changed to the women who had rearranged both of their lives forever. Frenic told how he and Sherry had tied the knot the year before. He said they would have done it sooner but she was holding out for her brother's return. Frenic told Bubba that she would have loved it if Bubba had given her away.

It was Bubba's turn to tell his new brother-in-law about the love of his life. He told him how they found one another, how they lived and how she died. The last part brought tears to his eyes. Something told Frenic that his wife's brother wasn't the same person lost years earlier. Bubba Lee was deeper and it seemed he had found his center.

Frenic changed the topic when he saw Bubba's grief boil up inside. "I guess you and I won't be fighting over your sister anymore. The minute she sees her namesake, we're both done for," Captain Frenic said laughing.

"I want to talk to you about that Tony. Sherry said I was jealous of you and acting childish. She was right on both accounts," Bubba confessed.

"That's all water under the bridge, said Frenic. "We are family, the four of us - well five counting that mutt of yours. If it helps, there's been more than one time she called me childish. I think it's a man thing, you know."

The sun was high over head when the Captain of the freighter looked at his watch. "Bubba I hate to cut this short but we are in a bit of a rush; the storm last night put us behind and off course. How long before you could be ready to set sail?" the Captain asked.

"Not long, I would ask you to allow me to visit my Nasus so we can say our final goodbyes," said Bubba. It was a request no one could deny.

Bubba took his daughter to the clearing where his Nasus was buried while their things were being transported to the ship. The entire island had been ravaged by the storm, all but Nasus's clearing. It had been untouched and appeared as it was the last time they had visited. Bubba took it as a good sign; maybe it was Nasus reaching from the grave to give her blessing.

He spoke to her in nearly a whisper, telling her he would never forget his island princess and he would make sure their little one wouldn't either. He told her how much he loved her and time couldn't change that. Lastly he said that when it came his time to go, he would be laid next to her, and maybe heaven had an island where they could be forever.

It was late afternoon when Bubba and his party made it back to the dingy. Frenic had already gone back to the ship to make preparations for his honored guest. Two men awaited their return.

"Well my little princess, this is it. There's a great big world out there and it's time you saw some of it," the little girl's father told her as he sat her in the small craft. "Come on Jester, you're next," Bubba hollered. He then helped the two men push the dingy out to sea.

Bubba sat facing the island as the men rowed them to the ship. He watched as the island became smaller and smaller. It reminded him of another time, years before, when he watched another island slip from sight.

"Goodbye my love," he whispered silently.

A hero's welcome awaited the castaways aboard the freighter. All the men were lined up on the upper deck waiting to catch sight of the legend. Few had ever met the man, but all had heard stories of the famed, Captain Cowboy.

The welcoming came as a nice surprise to Bubba Lee. He had no idea that he and Jester were part of the island folklore. Every eye was on him and his company as they boarded the ship. One man even asked him to sign a book.

"What's this?" he said as he handed Little Sherry to her new uncle. "Captain Cowboy and Jester" Bubba read the cover. "Who in the.....?" Then he saw the author's name. "Doc, you wait till I catch up with you.

"That ought to be easy enough, he's living in your house," Captain Frenic filled him in.

"Captain I have what you requested," a little man said coming from the galley.

"It ain't as good as your sister's but I imagine it's been some time since you've had some ice tea," Frenic explained handing him the glass. The Captain knew offering Bubba his first glass of ice tea was like offering any other man his first shot of whiskey.

"Now if I just had a dip of snuff, I'd be in high cotton," Bubba Lee remarked. The sailors all cheered as he took a drink.

The moment Bubba set foot on the boat, everyone, including Frenic, referred to him as Captain McBride. He took it as a sign of respect but it had been years since he thought of himself as such.

Bubba's daughter and dog were taken below deck after a while.

"I'm sorry Bubba but the doctor will have to examine you and Little Sherry. Company policy and the like," Captain Franic said with a smile. "While the doc gives you the once-over, I'll have the ship's steward prepare your state room. "I'll have him leave one of my uniforms for you and see what I can come up with for Little Sherry. I expect to see Captain McBride and his crew for dinner.""

"Tony, I can't thank you enough for everything but I need to ask one more thing of you. Would you see if my island has ever been charted? If not, would you do so. I can't bear to think about never visiting my Nasus again. And Tony, please don't tell my sister, I want to surprise her," Bubba asked of the Captain.

"I am already on the charts Captain. I'll have something for you after dinner," Frenic said with a smile. "And you are damn sure going to surprise her; I just hope it don't put me in the doghouse. You and Little Sherry get settled in while I get this tub headed in the right direction"

The steward showed Bubba and his party to the Captain's quarters later on that night. He found the door was open and the ship's three officers were seated around the table. They all rose to their feet when the three castaways entered.

"Gentlemen, I give you Captain McBride and his crew. Captain you already know the ship's doctor and this is Steve Rogers, my second in command," Frenic said in a formal way.

"May I present my beautiful daughter and my first mate Jester to the officers of the ship," said Bubba proudly. "Gentlemen, please be seated."

Bubba had watched enough old movies where he could be formal and not sound like a hick. He gently seated Little Sherry in a home-made booster chair the ship's steward brought to him And Jester found a bowl of warm gravy waiting for him on the floor.

Bubba just took it all in. The night before, they were in a cave waiting out the storm. Life was just as much a carnival ride as it was the day he and Jester waited on the docks for Jim Moore and his sea plane.

"How about a T-bone Captain, I'll bet it's been awhile," Frenic offered as the cook brought a platter of food.

"Where in the world did you get your hands on such prime cuts?' Bubba wanted to know.

"You forget my wife has a café. Once a month we'll sneak in and get a case out of the cooler," Frenic confessed.

"In other words you get them the same place I used to get mine. Believe me Captain Frenic, she is fully aware of your 'hijinks,' just as she was mine," Bubba said laughing.

Captain Franic stood up saying, "I propose a toast gentlemen to Captain Bubba Lee McBride. He's one of a kind."

"Sir, you have my gratitude, but I am no more a Captain today as I was the day the Texas Ship of Fools went down. I was just a man with a boat that thought I could do anything. Now I don't even have a boat," Bubba humbly explained to his host.

"I beg to differ with you Captain McBride. Not many seamen I know could sail a small boat through the heart of the storm of the century and live to tell the story. Not many men I have met have the stones.

"And you do have a boat. Captain Boulet left the Deliverance with Sherry for a day like today: the day Captain Cowboy sails again," Frenic enlightened his brother in-law.

"What of Boulet," Bubba asked.

"No one knows, Captain. They say he just wandered off one day," was the Captain's answer.

The meal was coming to a close; stories had been told and toasts drank. Bubba asked the doctor if he would mind watching after Little Sherry while he and Captain Frenic talked. The doctor said it would be his pleasure to see after the child.

The room belonged to the two sea Captains. Frenic's first mate had taken his watch on the bridge while Bubba's first mate was asleep on the floor.

"Bubba I can't offer you a dip of snuff, but I do have some fine Cuban cigars," the Captain offered and Bubba took him up on the offer.

The Captain closed the door to his quarters so he and Bubba could speak in private.

"About your island Bubba, we cannot find any record of it anywhere, but we have plotted its location. I have a brother with a high-dollar law degree and I will have him look into it. Chances are if there is no claim on it, it belongs to you. The good Lord knows you lived there long enough. But to file a claim, I need you to name it," Frenic explained.

"The Island of Nasus," Bubba responded without even thinking about it.

"There is one other thing we need to discuss this evening. I wish I had it in my power to turn this tub around and take you home. God knows I would love to see the look on your sister's face when you appear. Unfortunately I have deadlines and commitments to keep," said the Captain.

"It would be foolish of me to ask you and Little Sherry to stay with us until we make home port; that is three weeks away. A freighter is no place for a little girl. Hell, it doesn't take a genius to figure that out. It is where I asked my own wife to come aboard. You'd be a damn fool if you didn't want to get home as quickly as you could, I don't think there's a damn thing foolish about you Captain McBride.

"We make port tomorrow on an island to take on more cargo. I have a man there that has a helicopter service. He's crazy as a bed bug but he's a damn fine pilot. Come to think of it, he's a Vietnam vet too. Crazy Davis is what they call him," Frenic informed Bubba.

"Lt Col. Davis - we called him the rocket man, said Bubba about what he knew about the man. "You're right he is nuttier than a fruit cake. I didn't know him in Nam, but I heard of him, hell everyone in the

254

country heard of him. He had a top-of-the-line P.A. system mounted on his helicopter. He'd fly through the jungle playing Purple Haze or CCR full bore. It would scare the living shit out of Charlie."

"Ain't much changed, he still flies over the ocean sometimes with his music wide open," Captain Frnic offered. "It drives the cruise ships crazy. Anyway he owes me a favor and I thought I'd asked him to fly you and Little Sherry home, if you don't mind."

"That fine with me, I've always wanted to meet the crazy son-of-a-bitch anyway," Bubba replied.

The two men talked an hour or so more before Frenic told his guest it was time for him to hit the rack. Bubba thanked him for the supper and all his kindness. He told his brother-in-law goodnight but not before snagging another one of those fine Cuban cigars. He called to Jester, and topside they went.

Bubba needed a minute just to take in the day. He lit his smoke and took a long drag. The day had been nearly picture perfect. It would have been perfect if only Nasus was by his side. Perhaps she was, how else could he had gotten so lucky that day. He took one last drag, stamped it out and went down below to find his daughter.

Bubba woke the next morning and found the bunk next to him was empty. Little Sherry and Jester were both missing. He scrambled to get his pants on and when he got in the hallway, he saw the ship's steward.

"Have you seen my daughter and my dog this morning," he asked the man. "And would you have the time?" Bubba followed up.

"Your little girl is with the Captain in the galley; I believe he is introducing her to a bowl of oatmeal. It is nearly 10 a.m. sir. The Captain said to let you sleep because you must be exhausted. I can take you to the galley," the steward offered and Bubba took him up on it.

Bubba saw his daughter on her knees on a stool, shoveling oatmeal in her mouth as fast as she could. Her uncle Tony was laughing about as hard as she was shoveling.

"Hell Tony, you done stole my sister, now you want my daughter," Bubba joked.

"You rested well, I hope?" Frenic asked with a smile.

"Like a baby. You haven't seen Jester around have you," Bubba asked.

"I believe he and Mr. Rogers are topside. Comparing notes no doubt, you know one first mate to another," the Captain informed him

Bubba laughed as he could almost picture it in his mind.

"How would you like the cook to fix you some bacon and eggs?" Frenic then asked.

"You read my mind, you know how long it has been since I've had a fried egg," Bubba stated.

Captain Frenic told the old cowboy he was kinda liking the "Uncle Tony" bit. He also told Bubba he and Sherry had been considering having a child. Bubba told him to hurry because Little Sherry needed someone to grow up with. Frenic thought that was a good argument and that he'd try it out and see if she would bite.

"We'll be in port in a few hours. I've already contacted Davis. He said he had a charter this morning, but he could fly you and yours home tonight. He had heard of you as well in Nam. Davis said he'd consider it an honor to fly a fellow soldier home.

He handed Bubba a credit card. "You take this. I don't want an argument about it. You buy you and Little Sherry whatever you need while you wait for

Davis. Consider it six years of Christmas and birthday presents, or you can consider saving my ass. If I sent you home to your sister looking like you've just been rescued off a deserted island, she'd have my ass," Captain Frenic reasoned.

"Daddy, daddy, Uncle Tony said I could have a pony. Daddy, what's a pony?" the little girl asked.

The two men laughed then Frenic explained that the year Bubba Lee had been lost, Sherry had gone back to Texas and bought him a horse for his birthday. He told Bubba that everyone had said it would be a long shot if she ever saw you again, so she named the horse Long Shot. The story warmed Bubba's heart.

Bubba had just enough time to take a quick shower and stop by the sick bay where a man cut his hair. He looked in the mirror and saw his former self. He just hoped he would not scare Little Sherry. He had nothing to worry about; she just laughed at the new and improved look of her daddy.

The ship made port about the time he finished making himself presentable. Captain Frenic and his crew waited above deck to send their castaways off. Bubba appeared from the hatch holding his little girl's hand. Jester was a step behind sporting a new bandana that one of the crew had slipped around his neck.

"I can't thank the Captain and crew enough. You have freed me and my dog, and made it possible for my daughter to have a life. Once again I think you all," Bubba said as he faced the crew.

Captain Frenic shook his brother in-law's hand after escorting him down the gang plank. He had arranged a guide for Bubba and introduced them once they were ashore.

"You give my wife a kiss for me and tell her the rest was your idea," Frenic said.

"Covering your behind, like a true married man," Bubba fired back.

"You bet," was the last thing Bubba heard the man say.

Frenic and his crew went about the task of loading cargo into the hole. Bubba and his contention disappeared into the crowded docks.

Their guide first took them to where they could get some lunch. The word spread through the small village that the famed Captain Cowboy had been found, while they ate some fish tacos. A crowd began to gather outside the small fish shack. Whispers spread through the people when one would catch sight of them.

Bubba tried to pay the man once they had finished the meal. The owner would not accept his money. He had a funny feeling his guide also doubled as a reporter. He found hundreds of island folk outside the eatery.

The people followed them from store to store. Each time he tried to pay for what they wanted, the store clerks wouldn't take his money. The three castaways were treated like royalty. Bubba couldn't help but be touched by their kindness. He never dreamed he would be a legend anywhere, for anything. He was sure to thank the people for each act bestowed on them.

It was true all the islands were beautiful, the Lord's masterpieces. The people who called the islands their home were just as much his work of art.

A car was waiting after their day of shopping was behind them. It took the new arrivals down a dirt road that lead to an old airstrip. On the way, Bubba reflected on the day, it was one for the memory books. He just knew Nasus had been watching from on high.

He began to think about his island, the one he hadn't seen in years. Bubba wondered what had changed since he'd been gone. His home was no longer any particular place. That was one thing he had learned from Nasus. "Home is where you are loved and cherished" he thought to himself.

Bubba saw an old familiar sight, one he hadn't seen since the war: a vintage Huey helicopter. They were known as the Jolly Green during the war. Some said the old Huey was the finest machine Bell Helicopter ever made.

Bubba retrieved his haul from his day of shopping and began to make his way toward the aircraft. Little Sherry and Jester followed from behind. He could tell the day had worn his daughter out. She was in need of a nap.

The closer he came to the helicopter, the more his spirits began to fall. He saw a man covered with grease looking as though he was plenty mad. He'd work a minute then he'd throw his tools. He'd say some choice words then retrieve his tool. It would have been funny if Bubba wasn't in a hurry.

"You damn piece of no good government junk. I should have scrapped you out years ago," Bubba heard as he approached.

"Col. Davis, I'll take it," Bubba muttered.

"Hello folks, if it ain't the man of the hour," Davis said as his mood changed.

"I take it our trip has been put on hold?" Bubba wanted to know.

"Whatever gave you that idea, McBride," the pilot said as though he and the cowboy went way back.

"I don't know Colonel, maybe the boxed-end wrench chunked half way down the airstrip.," he pointed out.

Don't worry, that's just me and her having a lover's spat. We go through it often, just part of having a thirty-year-old helicopter," Davis mused. "You give me a few hours and she'll be good as new," he added.

"I'll give you a hand if you have a place I can bed my daughter down for a spell; her battery is about gone," Bubba stated.

"Sure thing, we can put her in the office, I have an extra pair of overalls in there," Davis said, granting his request.

The man made a bed for Little Sherry while Bubba put on the overalls. Jester curled up beside the little girl just as he had done every day of her life. She was asleep before her head ever hit the make-shift pillow and her four-legged babysitter was right behind her in that respect. Bubba took a passing glance before following the pilot out the door.

Bubba sat on a five-gallon oil can while the man worked his magic. "Where did you ever find this old bird?" Bubba asked.

"Find her, hell I stole her. They gave me my discharge papers and expected me to ride a C-130 home. Shit, I jumped in this old bitch and hopped, skipped and jumped my ass all the way here. I figure they'd just leave her behind anyway. They never came looking for her at any rate,"

Bubba was taken by the half-crazed chopper pilot, so much so that he began to open up. "You know Colonel, people have treated me all day like some kind of hero. I ain't no damn hero, I'm just a fool who got lost," he confided.

"It's karma man, that's what it is," Davis responded.

"For what?" Bubba looked puzzled.

"I had a buddy that was shot down in Nam. He was hunted down like a dog by the Vietcong. They throw his ass in POW camp and for two years they tortured this poor bastard. He was on the verge of offering himself when this wild-ass Texan and his platoon busted down the gates and raided the hooches.

"Thirty-one POW's were saved from what he told me was certain death. The name of that wild-ass Texan, I believe, was Sergeant McBride. I never heard of anyone throwing you a parade over that, now did they? Enjoy it my friend, you've earned it." The pilot made his point.

"It was a good day, that day," was all Bubba could say.

The sun had disappeared from the sky and darkness filled the night. It was a little past ten when Davis gave the go-ahead. Bubba secured his daughter and his pooch before giving Davis the thumbs up. Slowly but surely the old war horse lifted off the ground.

Little Sherry began to cry when she heard the sounds and felt the shaking of the Huey fight against gravity. Bubba took her in his arms to comfort her. She was asleep before long, knowing she was safe.

Jester rested his head on Bubba's lap. He stroked the dog with his free hand. "This has to be a record for a dog, Jester. You've rode in a pickup, car, plane, raft, zip line, and now a helicopter. You are one traveling S.O.B. you know that boy," he said to his faithful companion.

Jester joined Little Sherry in dreamland, leaving Bubba alone with his thoughts. He wondered if Sherry still left the neon light on for him and Jester. He wondered what became of Captain Boulet and why he would leave all he loved behind. It didn't make a lick of sense. He released the thought after studying on it; it was going to take more than a half-baked cowboy to figure out Captain Brian Boulet.

He then turned to his plan of action, how he was going to give them a surprise they wouldn't soon forget.

It was after three a.m. when the lights of Bubba's island came into view. One of his early questions was answered right away. Bubba could see the flash of the Yellow Rose's neon sign a mile out.

"Look Jester, it won't be long now," Bubba told the dog.

"Is there anywhere particular you want me to land this bird," Col. Davis asked.

"Can you set her down on the far end of the docks?" Bubba said pointing his finger in the direction.

"Roger that, Captain Cowboy," the old pilot said with a smile.

Davis cut the engines as soon as the wheel touched the surface of the docks. Bubba woke Little Sherry and freed Jester from his restraints. He was home, home at last and there was no feeling like it in the world.

Davis said he was going to grab some sack time if he was no longer needed. Bubba thanked the man and invited him to the world's best breakfast when he woke up. Bubba set off down the pier in the direction of his first victim.

Captain Frenic had confided that Jon Carpenter had taken to living on the Deliverance. He even went as far as telling his brother in-law the number of the slip. He had rehearsed what he was going to do a half dozen times in his head. He was going to take full advantage of being the newest haunt.

It wasn't long before he had the craft in his sights. Silently he stepped over the railing and then called to Jester. Bubba led the dog down the hatch to where he knew his old buddy was sleeping.

He found the door leading to the Captain's stateroom in no time. Bubba entered the darkness of the room where he heard Carpenter snoring. He found a chair by a lamp in the corner. Bubba sat in the chair with his daughter on his knee.

"Go ahead Jester, you remember how to do it. Wake Jon up," Bubba commanded.

Jester and all hundred and eighty pounds of him jumped in the middle of the bed and began to lick the man's face.

"Damn it Bubba, call Jester off. I'm sleeping," the man said in his sleep.

Carpenter then opened his eyes and looked straight into Jester's. Suddenly it dawned on him he wasn't dreaming. Scared out of his wits, he moved quickly to the front of the bed, clinging to his covers like a small child. He tried desperately to gain his senses by rubbing his eyes as fast as he could.

"Jester, bullshit, I have to be dreaming," he told himself. "How did you get here?" the man asked in case he wasn't dreaming.

Bubba turned on the lamp beside him.

"Boo! How in the hell do you think Jester got here. I drove him all the way from the spirit world," said Bubba, springing the remainder of his joke.

An ice-cold shiver ran down Carpenter's spine. His eyes grew to be the size of silver dollars after seeing the friend he had long since given up. The shadow of the light on Bubba's face just added to the haunting.

"No Jon, you're not dreaming, and I ain't no freaking ghost," Bubba said damn near ready to bust a gut.

It took a while for the man to come to grips with the fact that his best friend was looking at him and more importantly, he was alive. Carpenter remained speechless trying to add up the situation. A million thoughts ran like a wild fire through his brain. Each thought had at least ten questions attached to it and they were all trying to come out at the same time.

"Well hell, say something. It's not every day I get to come back from the dead," Bubba said laughing.

Carpenter noticed the little girl sitting on her daddy's knee. It was more than adding insult to injury; it was stacking confusion on top of confusion. "What's that you got on your lap?" the man said stuttering.

"This old friend, this is my daughter. Say hello to Uncle Scaredy Cat, Little Sherry," Bubba said unable to control his laughter.

Bubba's answer posed a whole new set of questions for the man. He tried to answer some at first but there were just too many.

"I'll tell you what, when we round everybody up, I'll tell everyone the complete story," Bubba said.

"You get your ass dressed and go get Doc. I got a bone to pick with him anyway. Meet me at the Yellow Rose, we are gonna give little sister a surprise she won't forget," Bubba instructed.

"Bubba. I went to bed the Captain of the Deliverance. I woke up taking orders from a spook," Carpenter stated.

"I know, ain't life a carnival," Bubba said with a laugh. Bubba gathered up his daughter and called to Jester once he told Carpenter the plan. The party of three made their way to the main gate of the Marina. Bubba was looking down while saying something to the dog when he nearly ran over a large object in the middle of his path.

"What the...? This wasn't here before. What the hell is it," he asked out loud.

He shined the flashlight that he had stole from the boat on his stumbling block. He saw himself looking back at him. It was the statue Sherry had commissioned years before. A lump rose in his throat when he read what was written on the base of his and Jester's likeness.

"Damn boy, it looks like we have a few surprises headed our way. I must say you look pretty good for an old dog," Bubba said trying not to get choked up too much.

They continued down the cobblestone road after the short pause at the statue. The sleepy little hamlet was still in slumber when its most famous, adopted son walked down her streets with his child and old Jester. The village would come to life with the business of the day in a few hours.

It had been some time since Saint Renee had been awakened like they would be that day. Bubba's idea was to surprise his sister, tell his story and then slip off to a peaceful place. He wanted to ease back into island life. He wondered if that was even a reasonable expectation.

It wasn't long before they stood beneath the flashing neon light of the Yellow Rose. Bubba shifted little Sherry from one hip to the other so he could retrieve the key from his pocket. It had stayed with him through everything. He never knew if he would ever be able to use it again.

"Now let's see if the thing still works," he said in a whisper. Bubba slipped the key in and turned it. The tumbler caught and the lock released. He turned the knob and the door opened. The scent of the night's cooking still hung in the air. It was one of the smells he had missed the most. He took a deep breath and filled his lungs with the heavenly aroma.

The first thing Bubba noticed was his old hat hanging on its nail. "Damn thing beat me back," he mused.

He removed it and gave it the once over. It had been cleaned and reblocked. The tag was still inside. "Capital Hatters, Stephenville, Texas," he read out loud. "I guess Chuck was locked up or something. It's all good, James did a fine job," he said because he knew most of the hatters in Texas.

Bubba took the hundred percent, pure beaver hat and put it on. "Finally, now I am fully dressed," he claimed to an empty café.

He looked around the place; not much had changed since he and Jester had been gone. He noticed a glass display case that he didn't remember. He walked to it still carrying Little Sherry. The case was filled with Bubba's life; all but the last six years.

He saw pictures of him and Sherry dating back to childhood, his metals from Vietnam and the buckles he had won at the rodeo. Jester's silver dog bowl had its special place, as did Bubba's tea-stained fruit jar.

It was the jar that grabbed his attention. It was the same fruit jar he had traded his shot glass in for. He remembered the day his drinking career came to a stop; it was the same day he got Jester. He removed it from the displays case with the soul intention of putting it to use as soon as possible.

He noticed several framed pictures over the display case, pictures he had never seen. A picture of the cooks from the 3-C Ranch was the first. He wondered how in the hell Ben and Rodney got the chuck wagon to the island.

The second picture was of a stage with Brian Burns and Larry Joe Taylor performing. The last picture was of a huge crowd around the statue he had almost run into earlier. "It must have been one hell of a party, I'm half sorry I missed it," he said with a laugh.

Little Sherry was getting restless in her daddy's arms. Bubba scanned the room until he saw the high chair in the corner. It was the same high chair he remembered from his youth. It was Sherry's high chair; the woman never got rid of anything.

Bubba placed his daughter in the chair and then fumbled with the bag on his shoulder. Inside were the toys the island people had given her the day before. He placed them on the tray in front of her. Outside he could hear two voices coming up the street.

"I can't believe you got me out of a dead sleep. I tell you Jon it was a dream. I guess I am just as crazy. Here I am in the wee hours of the morning coming to look at your dream," a voice said. Bubba knew the voice belonged to Doc.

"You'll see soon enough. It's Bubba, Jester, and a baby," came Carpenter's voice.

"You see Jon, you lost me on the baby. Where in the hell did baby come from?" the person behind the voice wanted to know.

"I'm having a little trouble with that myself, but he said he would explain it to us," Carpenter explained.

Doc turned the knob to the door of the Yellow Rose and to his surprise the thing opened.

"Well hello Doc. It's sure good to see you. Jon, be careful what you say around this feller, you'll end up in a book somewhere," Bubba said giving the man one of his looks.

Doc began looking around the room. "What are you looking for," Carpenter asked.

"Oh nothing, I just wondered if Bubba brought the King back with him," the man laughed.

"Little Sherry, do you remember your Uncle Scardy Cat? This is your other uncle, Uncle Tell All,"

273

Bubba said, referring to the book he had seen two days before.

"Damn Bubba, everybody had you as stink bait and here you were making babies. I want to see you explain this to your sister," Doc fired back.

"It's a good story, but like I told Jon, you'll have to wait for Sherry. Meanwhile will one of you tell me about that over-sized paper weight in the middle of the road. The damn thing almost mugged me on the way up here," he stated.

"Oh yeah, I think it's best to let your sister explain that one. I always thought it looked like a hobo and his flea-bitten mutt," Carpenter said, trying to get even for the manner in which he was invited to the party.

The three men were laughing and joking when the smallest person in the room interrupted. "Daddy, I'm hungry," the little girl cried.

"Not to worry baby girl, Daddy's on the job. Do you think you two could manage to keep an eye on her while I go rustle up a little grub. It ain't as good as my sister's but hell, she ain't here," Bubba said directing the question to the two men.

Bubba headed for the swinging doors leading into the kitchen. He turned back to find his friends talking baby talk to the little girl. "I wonder just who's watching who," he asked Jester. "Let see if we can't find you a bone or two," he continued once they had disappeared behind the doors.

It wasn't long before the little girl had captured the hearts of the grown men. They were so caught up in their peek-a-boo, that they nearly failed to see Sherry coming up the street.

"Oh boy; here comes Big Sherry," Doc said, coining the phrase.

"This is fixing to get interesting," Carpenter said after seeing her.

They agreed quickly they were not going to say a word, they'd let their old friend explain it all. It seemed like the least they could do.

"What did I do, forget to lock the …..?" her voice tapered off when she saw Doc, Carpenter and the little girl. "Does someone have a secret they would like to get off their chest," she asked seeing the little girl.

Both men shook their heads "no."

"Then would one of you explain why you two are in here with a child this early in the morning?' She never gave them a chance to answer. "You're so prett. What's your name and why are you with these two bums?" she asked the little girl.

"Sherry," the child said.

"That's sweet you taught her to say my name," Sherry said.

"How we going to do that, we can't even get her to say our names," Carpenter grumbled.

"No, that is her name. And no, she does not belong to me or Jon. Her daddy's in the kitchen." Doc pointed out.

The shit really hit the fan when she heard they had allowed a complete stranger in her kitchen.

"What! Both of you know better. I'm getting to the bottom of this. I'll deal with you two later. Watch the little girl," she said as she stormed off toward the kitchen. Whoever was in her kitchen was fixing to get a good chunk of her mind.

"This ought to be fun," Carpenter told Doc.

"Yeah, I just hope no one gets killed in the process. With her temper it's highly possible," Doc reasoned.

The man in the kitchen was digging around in the ice box with his back to her. She couldn't tell much about him like that. Her blood pressure began to rise automatically because the man was wearing her brother's hat. She knew he wasn't from Saint Renee; everyone there knew that hat was off limits.

She was at her breaking point and about to blow when she heard, "Damn it, I can't find anything. She's gone and moved it all around."

She knew the voice but it couldn't be. She felt Jester's cold nose on the back of her hand and saw the massive dog. She knew. Bubba Lee turned to find her standing behind him.

"You're early! Hey sis, where are you keeping the bacon these days?" Bubba asked as though the past six years never happened.

Big tears of joy began to swell up in her eyes. Bubba couldn't play his little game any longer. He had dreamed about that one moment for years. He put his arms around her and she buried her face in his chest.

Everything was fine up until she pushed him away. "Bubba Lee, you son-of-a-bitch; just where in the hell have you been. Didn't it matter that you had someone who missed you and cried herself to sleep for years. Were you too busy making babies to think of me. Every day for six freaking years I've lived with the fear someone was going to show up with your body. Damn you for putting me through this," she said, letting him have it.

"Are you done?" answered Bubba. "Now you hear me and hear me good little sister. I am surprised at you; you know me better than that. I didn't stay lost because I wanted to. Every day I knew you were worried sick but there wasn't a lot I could do. The one thing I was sure of was you weren't going to give up hope, so neither did I. Your love kept me going.

"Now if you'll calm down and help me fix breakfast, I'll tell you about the last six years of my life. I'll give you a preview before I tell Doc and Jon. By the way, your husband says hello." He knew that would get her back hairs up but he couldn't resist having a little more fun.

"You mean you've seen Tony, my God how is it I am the last to find out you are alive?" Sherry demanded to know.

"What can I say, I save the best for last. Besides I seriously doubt if you ever thought I was dead. I know you about as well as you know me, little sister," Bubba explained.

He began to tell her his story, starting where her husband had found them and worked his way backwards. Sherry hung on her brother's every

278

word. Bubba was a better story teller than he was a cook so he let her do the cooking while he told the story.

He had stopped for a moment when it came to the part about Nasus. Sherry could see the hurt in his eyes when he spoke of his late wife.

Tears began to run down his face when he told Sherry about the day his Nasus died. "Damn onions, do it to me every time," he said trying to hide his emotions.

Sherry felt her brother's loss and stopped what she was doing and hugged him. She looked out the opening into the dining room where Little Sherry was being amused by the two men.

"She sure is a beautiful child. Her Aunt Sherry is going to take good care of her and her Daddy.

"Yep, she's a little princess like her momma," Bubba said, brushing away his tears.

"Bubba you know I never gave up hope but those two men kept me going at times. You and I are blessed with good friends," she told him. "And I never gave up on you either, Jester," she said bending down and hugging him.

Breakfast was ready by the end of Bubba's story.

"It's about time! What did you have to do, gather the eggs by yourself? We were about ready to take this pretty little thing to the mainland for breakfast," Carpenter said in his usual outspoken way.

"I could just see the two of you on the mainland with a little girl - you talk about a three ring circus," Sherry snapped back.

"I'd buy a ticket to see that show," Bubba chimed in.

Bubba Lee filled his plate with her "devine" cooking. He put a fork full in his mouth and closed it with great pleasure. "Damn sis, you ain't lost a step."

It was hard to tell if she even heard his compliment; she was busy helping Little Sherry with her breakfast.

"Well boys, I ain't been in town two hours and I've already lost my daughter," he said in between his mouthfuls of his sister's cooking.

"I wouldn't worry about it none. Sherry did a pretty good job with you and she had a whole lot less to work with," Carpenter mentioned, trying to even the score over some of Bubba's teasing.

Col. Davis came in about halfway through the meal. "Come on in Colonel, pull up a chair and wrap your mouth around this chow," Bubba said, introducing and inviting the pilot to breakfast.

Bubba waited until everyone was finished before telling his story. He started by saying it might be the truest story he ever told. Sherry had already heard the tale but didn't mind the rerun. He left parts of it out because those were his precious memories. All in all, everyone agreed it was a good story.

Sherry's staff had all arrived by the time Bubba brought his story to its conclusion. "Boys would you grant me one favor, would you two take my daughter up to the house and let her catch a little sleep. I fear this morning has plumb tuckered her out," he asked of his two friends. "I would like a long walk with my sister, if she has a mind to."

"I don't know old buddy, I seem to remember something was said about a three-ring circus and buying tickets," Carpenter said in a playful voice.

"I'll put it like this: if you two want something else to eat, you'll go lay this child down," Sherry shot back.

"Well McBride, I'll guess I'll take my leave. Sounds like you are home to me," Col. Davis said.

"Yes he's home alright, even though it's a very dysfunctional home," Sherry said as she thanked the man for bringing her brother home.

"I swear Doc, I went to bed a sea Captain last night, now look at me, I'm a nanny," Carpenter muttered as he and Doc walked out the door.

A few moments later Sherry and Bubba were walking arm in arm down the cobblestone street. The village was just waking up so the full force of the return of Captain Cowboy had yet to hit.

Tell me dear brother, do you have any plans? Any new adventures for you and the crew?" she asked of her brother.

"I want a big house with a wrap-around porch. I want to sit in my rocking chair and watch my dog grow old and my daughter grow up. I am done with adventure," he told his sister.

"Yeah right, that will last about a week," she laughed.

"I guess you're probably right," he agreed as they walked into the morning sun.

CPSIA information can be obtained at www.ICGtesting.com
Printed in the USA
LVOW120628021211

257515LV00001B/1/P